Derek's Darling Damsel

All the President's Men, Volume 2

Rose Nickol

Published by Rose Nickol, 2021.

This is a work of fiction. Similarities to real people, places, or events are entirely coincidental.

DEREK'S DARLING DAMSEL

First edition. April 16, 2021.

Copyright © 2021 Rose Nickol.

ISBN: 979-8201253110

Written by Rose Nickol.

Chapter One

Derek Moore started The Mix, a BDSM club in Quantico, Virginia, with three other former Secret Service agents, Tyler Thomas, Link Davis, and Trent Clark, three years ago. The club was very popular. The group started it because they were all thinking of retiring within the next five years and wanted something to fall back on.

Working for the Secret Service, they all were on the same team and great buddies. The club was something they had talked about for years and was now a reality. It was the only one in the area and people came from miles around. Membership was limited and there were very strict rules that were followed. They were all close to retiring and the club seemed like the perfect thing to do next.

The assignments Derek received as a Secret Service agent were usually boring, and tonight had proven to be no exception until the arrival of Ms. Dorothy Chapman.

Derek Moore was forty-two years of age and ready to find someone to settle down with. None of the women he had been with were interested in a long-term relationship, preferring to play at the club and an occasional date, but nothing more. Not that it bothered him, he hadn't found anyone he really wanted to spend his life with.

At six feet eight inches and almost three hundred pounds, he was very intimidating. He often scared women off. They didn't know what a teddy bear he could be. Except when he was in the club. He was very strict and used his intimidating size to his advantage with submissives and other dominants. He always got his way.

Tonight he was assigned to protect General Fredrico Alves. The General was very formal and had sent him into the hall almost two hours ago when the reporter from *The Washington Journal*, Dorothy (or Dottie as she liked to be called) Chapman had arrived. Since then no one had gone in or out of the room and it was very quiet. Almost too quiet.

Derek had seen Dottie at several functions and had spoken with her several times. She was the type of woman he could go for. She was tall, five feet ten inches at least, and had curves in all the right places. What his grandmother used to call "Rubenesque." Her full, lush breasts were made to fit in his huge hands. He had dreamed of sitting her on top of him and holding her plentiful hips while sucking her nipples. But other than politeness, she had never given him the time of day.

He remembered the look on her face as he gave her the standard pat-down before allowing her into the General's suite, it was a combination of disgust and lust. If he read her signals correctly, given the right circumstances, she wouldn't mind helping him make his dream come true.

He had another two hours before his relief arrived and he was more than ready. Maybe he could persuade little miss Dottie to join him for a drink in the hotel bar after his shift. That would be the perfect end to the night.

Imagining what else would make the night perfect, he thought he heard a muffled scream come from the General's suite. *What the hell?*

Pulling his gun, he called for backup and used his key to open the door. Looking around, he saw nothing out of place in the living room, and he didn't see the General or Dottie either.

Taking a risk, he called out, "General Alves, is everything okay?"

The General came out of the bedroom of the suite, wrapping a robe around what appeared to be his naked body.

"Mr. Moore, Ms. Chapman and I are—how do you say—otherwise occupied. Is there something I can help you with?"

"General, I thought I heard screams, is everything okay?"

"Yes, Mr. Moore. Ms. Chapman is a very passionate woman if you know what I mean."

"I'd like to talk to Ms. Chapman, myself, if you don't mind, General." Derek couldn't believe that Dottie would go willingly with this scum. As foreign ministers went, General Alves was bottom of the barrel. Short, fat, and ugly, Derek towered over the obnoxious little man.

"I don't think that is necessary, Mr. Moore. Ms. Chapman is resting and you wouldn't want to disturb her." The General answered and started guiding him to the door of the suite.

Just then, Derek heard another muffled scream. Pushing the General out of the way, he ran to the bedroom. What he saw there appalled and excited him.

Dottie Chapman was tied to the bed spread-eagle and gagged, naked. Derek quickly grabbed a blanket and covered her while doing his best to untie and ungag her.

"Is this how you treat reporters in your country, General?" Derek demanded. The scum was asking for it now and it was all Derek could do to keep from giving it to him.

The General merely shrugged, as if this were an everyday occurrence to him. Maybe it was.

Derek quickly talked into the microphone attached to his lapel as he unfastened the woman. Undoing the gag, he removed it and wiped the tears from her face with his thumbs. Pulling her to him, he held her, soothing and cuddling her. He had wanted Dottie in his arms, but this was not the way he had planned on doing it.

Within minutes, the room was full of people. Derek held Dottie and spoke softly to her.

"Honey I know this is hard, but I need to know, did he rape you?"

Dottie looked up at him and shook her head no. "But I think he was going to," she said softly with a sob.

Derek cupped her head with his hand and held it to his shoulder. Rocking her softly, one of the other members of his team, Tyler Thomas, came in and looked questioningly at him. Derek shook his head no. Tyler nodded and walked out.

What a fucking mess this had turned into. He had dealt with visiting dignitaries before, but none of them had been as bad as this ass.

They had to keep this fucking mess out of the press. Hopefully, Dottie would cooperate, but that could be dealt with later, now he needed to make sure she wasn't hurt and try to repair any damage he could.

"Baby, did he hurt you physically? Do you need to go to the hospital or see a doctor?" he gently asked her, holding her closer.

"No, no doctor, no hospital, please. He just tied me up and told me all the things he wanted to do." As she said this last, she visibly shuddered. "Please don't make me go to a hospital," she implored and looked up into his hazel eyes.

"Okay, no hospital. Will you let me take you to the room I have here and let me look and make sure you are okay?" he asked, holding her tighter if possible.

Sniffling, she nodded her head and relaxed into him. She had had a crush on Derek Moore since the first time she had seen him. He was pure muscle and built like a mountain. Tall and huge all over. He carried her like she was a feather. Not many men could do that. Having a crush at thirty-six was ridiculous, but she didn't know what else to call it.

Because of her job as correspondent to the White House, she and Derek mingled quite often, both of them having to be at the same functions. Every time she saw him, she creamed her panties, but she never saw any reaction from him. He was cool and polite, every bit the gentleman, and very distant. Even when he had patted her down before she entered the General's room, there was nothing but professionalism. She was sure he had no feelings for her. At times she didn't even think he noticed her.

And why would he? He was tall, very tall and built, a big, beautiful man, and she was...well...she was Dottie. Nothing special, nothing spectacular. She was tall for a woman and needed to lose a few pounds, but she didn't consider herself unattractive. She had had her share of dates over time and was definitely not a virgin, but Derek did something to her libido. Every time she was in the same room with him, her panties were damp even before he noticed her. What it was about him, she didn't know. Even now, if by some miracle he were to feel between her legs, he would find her wet.

What would he do if he noticed? Would he be disgusted? Would he be interested? Would she ever find out? What type of lover would Derek be? Would he be kind and gentle or fast and rough? She wanted to find out.

Dottie had heard that Derek and some of the other members of the service had opened a kink club called The Mix, but she didn't know anything about it. What type of kink was he into? Could she be enough for him?

Dottie had been so lost in her wonderings that she hadn't noticed Derek had stood up and was carrying her out of the room until she heard the General say, "It was almost a pleasure, Ms. Chapman, next time you won't be so lucky." Dottie shuddered and buried her face in Derek's shoulder.

"It will be you that won't be so lucky, General," Derek replied as he walked faster.

Due to the nature of the negotiations with the General's country, the entire floor of the hotel had been reserved for him, his staff, and the agents assigned to him. Derek's room was at the end of the hall. He walked quickly with Dottie, not wanting to expose her any more than necessary.

Shifting her so that he could hold her with one arm, he opened the door and carried her into his suite. "Can you stand a minute, baby?" he asked as he stood her on her feet.

Dottie grabbed onto his shoulders as he set her on her feet and secured the blanket around her. "I know this is difficult, but you need to tell me what happened. Are your clothes in the room?" He wanted her to be comfortable and knew she would feel better in her own things, even though the sight of her in the blanket did things to his cock. *Not now buddy,* he thought, *maybe soon, very soon.*

"He cut and tore my clothes. I'm sure nothing I have is wearable," she answered, pulling the blanket tighter around her.

"Okay sweetheart, we'll get you something. For now, wear this," he told her walking to the bedroom and coming back with one of his shirts.

Tucking the blanket so it was more secure, Dottie let him help her put the shirt on. Once she had it in place, he pulled the blanket away and knelt in front of her, buttoning the two middle buttons. When she went to do more buttons, he took her hands in his. "That's enough, baby, I like it that way," he told her with a soft growl in his voice.

Dottie looked down into his eyes and thought, *oh my*, thinking she needed someplace to sit before she fell.

Derek must have seen that her knees were weak and swept her back into his arms. He sat in an overstuffed chair, settling her into his lap. "Now tell me what happened," he said, kissing the top of her head.

Derek knew he was on dangerous ground. Having her in his lap was the best feeling, but not the smartest thing he could do. They both would have been safer if he had left her in the blanket, but she was beautiful in his shirt, and only his shirt. He needed to find out what had happened and report in. He knew the rest of his team would be handling the General, but they needed to know what they were working with, if the man was truly dangerous or just a pervert.

"Well, he was fine right after you left. We talked and I asked several questions, which he appeared to answer truthfully. He poured us each a drink, which I did not touch. That seemed to bother him. When he finished his drink, he asked me back to his bedroom, stating he wanted to show me a rare artifact that he had brought with him to give the president. Out of curiosity, I went. Stupid rookie mistake, I knew better. I should have never put myself in that situation. I know better, stupid, stupid, stupid." Tears started running down her face.

"Oh, baby, it wasn't stupid, you had no way to know what was going to happen. Can you tell me the rest?" Derek held her tighter and was soothing one hand over her thigh.

Taking a deep breath, Dottie went on, "Once he got me to the bedroom he pulled a knife out of his jacket. I remember his exact words. 'I suggest you sit on the bed, Ms. Chapman, we will talk more once you have.' Then he pushed me onto the bed and before I knew what had happened, he had my hands and feet tied to the bedposts. Then he gagged me. I tried to scream but couldn't get much sound out around the gag. You must have heard me though, thank you for saving me." She reached up and cupped his face, looking into his eyes with relief and something else—not gratitude, lust maybe?

Derek looked down into her face and couldn't help it, he brushed her lips with his. Dottie reached around and cupped his neck, pulling him closer and deepening the kiss. She parted her lips slightly and he slipped his tongue in, tightening his hold on her.

Cupping her head in both his hands, he held her tight and continued his assault on her mouth. When she parted her lips, he took the advantage and slipped his tongue inside, exploring every inch. She tasted so good. Kissing her was better than anything he had ever experienced. He wanted and was going to take more.

But first, he needed to find out what had happened in the General's room. He needed to inform his team, and then he would have the rest of his life to kiss her...and more.

Breaking the kiss, he pulled her close and, rubbing her back, said, "Dottie, tell me the rest of it."

Dottie took a deep breath and continued her story. "After he had me gagged and tied to the bed, he took the knife and started cutting my clothes. Once he had all my clothes removed, he sat on the side of the bed and started running the knife over my body. Then he told me all the things he wanted to do and removed his clothes." As she said the last, she again shuddered and buried her face in his shoulder, softly crying.

"That fucking bastard. He'll never get near you again, baby, and if by some fucking chance in hell he does, I will personally rip his balls off and stuff them up his ass." Derek growled as he held her tighter. He couldn't believe he had stood outside the suite and let all this happen. Some fucking guard he was. The General was lucky he still had his dick. Next time he wouldn't.

Loosening his hold on Dottie, he quickly spoke into the microphone on his chest. "Tyler, did you get all that?"

"Affirmative," the reply came back.

"I'm going off comm now. If you need me, don't bother. Briefing 8 a.m., Quantico."

"Affirmative," came the reply again. The one thing about working together as long as they had was that they needed very few words to communicate. Tyler knew of his feelings for Dottie and he was sure Tyler knew why he was going off comm and would make sure his evening was not interrupted. Business taken care of, he could focus on his woman now.

"Derek," she said hesitantly.

"Yes, baby?" he answered her.

"I want to take a shower, I need to wash the feel of his hands off of me." She was crying again.

"Of course, anything you want or need." He stood and walked to the bathroom with her. Luckily, this room was equipped with a huge walk-in shower and it would accommodate both of them.

Sitting her on the counter, he turned and started the shower to warm it. When he started removing his clothes, Dottie looked at him in alarm. "Wh–What are you doing?"

"I'm not leaving you alone. I'm coming in with you," he stated firmly.

"Thank you, but I think I can handle it," she answered.

"Not going to happen, I'm not leaving you alone." By now he had removed everything but his briefs and had turned to her.

His chest was massive and rippling. She wanted to run her tongue over every inch of it. Oh God, was all of him massive? Looking down at his briefs, she knew it was true. Even encased in the soft cotton fabric, she could tell he was huge. Would he ever fit inside her? She had a feeling she would be finding out sooner rather than later.

While she had been studying him, he had removed the shirt she was wearing and she was now naked again. Remembering how she got that way, she shuddered again and a tear slipped down her cheek.

Seeing the tear, Derek reached out and licked it off. "It's okay, you're safe with me. I won't hurt you and I won't do anything you don't want to do. Trust me," he said, lifting her and walking to the warm shower.

Setting her down in the running water, he quickly removed his briefs and followed her. Closing the door and encasing them in the steamy warmth, he noticed her staring at him. He was huge, bigger around than her wrist and long, pointing straight at her like a divining rod.

"Just ignore him, baby, he just wants some attention. He'll be fine," he said, referring to his cock.

"It's just so...big," she said reverently. She was in awe.

"Yeah, there's nothing small about me. Let's get you washed," he said grabbing the soap and lathering his hands.

"I can...oh," she said as he started rubbing his soapy hands over her back and buttocks.

He continued washing her, kneeling to lift her feet and wash each toe. Moving his hand up, he slid his hands up her leg using both hands to cup her leg, even though he could have wrapped one hand around them, until he came to the apex of her thighs. Looking up into her eyes, he parted her folds and leaned in, then licked from her back hole to her clit.

He felt her shudder and put his hands on her hips to steady her. "Okay?"

"Oh God, yes, don't stop," she groaned when another tremor ran through her.

"I'll make it good for you. Hold onto my shoulders." He felt her brace herself and lifted her other foot to give that leg the same treatment. Again when he reached her thighs, he took another lick.

Still kneeling, he lifted her and turned, sitting her on the built-in bench in the shower. "Spread your legs, love," he said, pushing her thighs apart and lifting her legs over his shoulders.

"Oh my God, I...don't stop." She was melting. When he took her clit in his mouth, her hips arched and she almost came off the bench. If he had not been holding her, she would have.

"Don't stop, oh...oh," she moaned, arching even more.

He used his hands to anchor her and ran his tongue around her little button. "Oh God, Dottie, you taste so good, and you're so hot, I may never stop." He grasped both buttocks in his hands and lifted her so that she was leaning back against the shower wall with her legs wide over his shoulders. Using his thumbs, he parted her and continued licking and sucking taking her higher and higher.

"Come for me. I want to feel you clench on my tongue and taste all your juices," he said just before he rolled his tongue and put it inside her.

She had never had anyone do what he was doing to her. The minute he put his tongue inside her, the dam broke and her juices flowed, coating his tongue and face.

Lapping at her like a small puppy, he drank everything she gave him, not letting her come down for what seemed like several minutes.

"Oh, Derek, what...oh my...Derek...I..." She couldn't put a coherent thought together. It just kept going and going until she thought she was going to pass out.

Finally, Derek pulled back and sat back on his heels, a satisfied grin on his face. Knowing he could take a woman to these heights with just his mouth was a personal victory. He wanted to stand and shout to the world that Derek Moore had made Dorothy Chapman come.

Still sitting with her legs over his shoulders, she leaned against the shower wall, panting, and trying to catch her breath. She didn't know what to call what she had had before Derek, but they definitely were not orgasms. This was mind-blowing. She wasn't sure her limbs were still attached, and she knew she wouldn't be able to walk.

Derek looked up at her a grin on his face. "You okay, baby?" he asked smugly.

"I'll never be okay again. That was, I don't even know how to describe it." She smiled and tried to move her legs.

"Oh, no, I'm not done yet," he growled and took her clit in his mouth.

"Ohhh, I don't think I can again," she moaned.

"You will, you will more than you ever thought you could," he said as he dove back in. When he had made her come twice more, he gently moved her legs back down and finished washing her, paying special attention to her beautiful breasts. He would be sucking on them soon.

He carried her out of the shower and dried both of them before carrying her into the bedroom and the king-sized bed. It wasn't as big as his bed at home, but it would have to do. Sitting on the side of the bed, he stood her between his legs, bringing her bountiful breasts right to mouth level.

"Put your hands on my shoulders and lean forward, love," he said, his voice dropping an octave and dripping with desire.

She did as he asked and he opened his mouth, taking as much of her breast inside as he could. Reaching around her, he grabbed both her buttocks in his hands and lifted her so that she was straddling him.

Moving his mouth, he instructed, "On, your knees," so that she was kneeling over his lap with her legs on the outside of his. Leaning back down, he took the other breast in his mouth, sucking and licking her ripe little berries.

"Oh, Derek, that's so good, don't stop." She moaned as he continued his licking and sucking. Moving her hands from his shoulders, she wrapped them around his head, pulling him closer.

"No, leave your hands on my shoulders." He groaned. He didn't want to restrain her after what had just happened, but he needed control.

"Oh, yes, don't stop," she moaned, not moving her hands.

"Put your hands back on my shoulders," he said just a little firmer this time.

"What...why...okay." She looked confused but did as he asked.

"That's my good girl, now where was I?" He took her breast back in his mouth and moved one hand between them to finger her clit. Her position was perfect and she was rocking back and forth on his cock, making him harder than he had ever been. He was going to have to take her soon.

Sucking and licking on her nipples, he had her writhing and moaning with need. "Is my baby ready for more?" he asked in a deep, intimate voice.

"More, oh my God, please." She panted back.

He flipped her around so that she was on her hands and knees on the bed. Getting a condom out of the bedside drawer, he quickly rolled it on then moved behind her. Leaning over her, he moved her long black hair off her neck and grabbed her tender flesh between his teeth.

He ran his hands over the globes of her full ass, slipping his thumbs into the crack, pressing one thumb firmly to her tiny hole.

"Oh, what...what are you doing?" she asked in a pant, trying to move her head.

"Just hold still, I'll make it feel good. I want you here, but not now. Now I'm going to take that beautiful pussy, and you are going to come like you never have before."

Oh my God, she thought, he already done that three times. Could it be any better? She didn't know but was more than willing to find out. This man knew exactly how to wind her up tighter than she ever had been. His controlling ways made her hotter than ever before. It was as if her body craved what he was doing and she wasn't scared at all. She wanted more.

Chapter Two

Dottie woke early the next morning. She was used to being up early to exercise before she needed to be at work and the fact that it was Saturday made no difference. Opening her eyes, she looked around. This wasn't her bedroom. All the events of the night before came back in a rush as she remembered everything that had happened. The bad and the good.

She needed to find clothes and get home. She was sure last night had been a mistake for both of them and just wanted to get home. Twisting and trying to get loose of Derek's grip, she rolled to face him.

Smiling down at her, he asked in a deep, sleep-filled voice, "Hey baby, what's up? You need the bathroom?"

Realizing that would get her up, she quickly nodded yes and he released her. She scooted out of the bed and ran for the bathroom. Once in there, she used the facilities and started a shower, wondering if she could find something besides a towel to wear.

Walking into the shower, she stood under the spray, trying to figure out how she had gotten in this situation. Derek had never shown the slightest interest in her before. What had happened last night? Did he just feel sorry for her and was he trying to comfort her after what had happened? Or was there something more there? Should she hope for more or just take what she had got and move on? How was she ever going to figure this out?

She was so busy replaying the part of the evening that had happened after they got to Derek's room that she didn't notice him entering the bathroom until the shower door opened and he strode in.

"Ack!" she screamed. "What are you doing?"

"Taking a shower, what are you doing?" he asked with a deep, sexy voice, and when he turned those hazel eyes on her, she melted.

"Oh...well...I thought." She tried to get out, but he grabbed her and pulled her to him.

"I didn't get my good morning kiss, bad girl," he said, fisting his hand in her hair and pulling her face up to meet his. Taking her lips in a bruising kiss, he released her hair, and cupping both her buttocks, lifted her to straddle him.

'Oh," she managed when he released her mouth to lean down and take a nipple. Adjusting her on him, he plowed inside her and started a pounding rhythm.

She hadn't noticed, but he walked into the shower wearing a condom, always prepared.

"We have to hurry, I have to be at Quantico at 0800 hours and I want you with me. We probably won't have time for breakfast but can grab coffee on the way, and there should be something there," he told her, the entire time bracing her against the shower wall and pounding her.

Lifting her by the hips, he quickly flipped her around until she was facing the shower wall, ass up. "Brace yourself, baby, this is going to be quick and rough," he told her as he pounded her harder and faster, drilling in and out.

"Oh my God, my clit, rub my clit," she moaned.

Wrapping one hand around her waist to hold her in place, he took the other hand and started pinching and pulling her clit. "Don't hold it back, scream for me. I want to hear you scream." He pounded her harder and faster, twisting and pulling her clit hard.

"Oh, oh, oh God," she screamed as she came. If she hadn't been braced against the wall with him holding her, she would have fallen flat on her face.

Still holding her around the waist, he lifted her until her feet no longer touched the floor and maneuvered them both to the bench in the shower. Sitting, he pulled her into his lap and let the warm water cascade over them for several minutes.

She relaxed into him, her body liquid. She knew she should move, but there was no way. Lying against him and letting the warm water wash away her cares, it was as if they were in their own little universe and nothing and no one could bother them.

Derek hated to move, but he had to be at the debriefing. Taking Dottie with him was probably a mistake, but he wanted the team to hear from her exactly what an ass the General was. Because of the negations that were happening, he knew his superiors would overlook the events of last night, but he needed to make sure nothing like that happened again. He would be glad when the ass went back to his own country and he was no longer a threat.

Standing with Dottie in his arms, he grabbed the soap and quickly washed both of them, and then he grabbed the shampoo and washed and conditioned her hair.

When he finished, he carried her out of the shower and dried them both, wrapping a towel around her and one around his own waist. He sat her in the chair at the vanity and grabbed a brush and the blow dryer.

"What are you doing?" she asked. No man had ever dried her hair.

"You want this dried, don't you? And if I don't brush it, you'll be full of tangles that we'll never get out."

"How do you know all that?" she asked incredulously.

"Sisters and a mother," he answered and turned the dryer on, brushing and drying her hair.

Once he had her hair dry, and she had to admit it looked good, he picked her up again and took her to the bedroom. Sitting her on the side of the bed, he walked out to the living room and came back with a small package.

Looking quizzically at it, she then looked up at him. "These should fit. If not, we'll find something else," he said as he handed the package to her.

She opened the package and found a pair of jeans and a shirt in her size. "How did you do this?" she asked. He hadn't left the room unless he snuck out while she was sleeping.

"One of the team found your things in the General's room, looked at the sizes, and went shopping."

"Wow, I thought I was going to have to wear a towel or one of your shirts home." She was shocked.

"Baby, you would look good in both of those or nothing at all, but I want you in a little more for the debriefing. You will find out I don't share what's mine. Ever. And you are mine." He growled.

"We have to get ready and head out or I would show you exactly what I mean, so if you don't want to walk out of the hotel naked, I suggest you get dressed."

Dottie took the package in her hands and pulled out the clothes. Looking through the package, she didn't find any underwear. Just the clothes. That's all. Nothing else. Looking again to make sure she didn't miss something, the bag was definitely empty.

"Uhm, Derek?" she called

"Yes, baby," he answered walking back from the closet now dressed in jeans and a black T-shirt.

"There's only a shirt and jeans here."

"What else do you need?"

"Underwear?" She made it a question. It should have been a demand.

"No." He answered her question blandly and sat on the bed beside her to put on his shoes and socks.

"What do you mean 'no'?" she asked.

"No. I have your shoes from last night. Let me finish and I'll get them. Are you going to put those on or just look at them? I really don't mind keeping you naked, but...the rest of the team might like it too much."

Dottie grabbed the clothes and stormed to the bathroom to get dressed. No underwear—what the hell was he thinking? Well, when she got home, she would fix that problem.

Dressing in what she had, she went looking for her shoes. Luckily, the General had just removed them and not done any damage, although she was sure that had it been necessary, Derek would have replaced those also. Derek even had her briefcase and purse from last night.

Even though she was still mad about the underwear, she looked up at him and smiled. He hadn't had to do all this for her. "Thank you." She reached up and cupped his face.

"You'll thank me better later. We have to go." He grabbed her hand and led her out of the room.

He took her out of the hotel a different way than she had come in and they went through a back door to a parking lot. There sat a black SUV. "Your chariot awaits, my lady," he told her as he opened the door and lifted her up.

They drove through Starbucks and got coffee and a Danish on the way to FBI headquarters.

"Why are we going to Quantico? That's FBI, aren't you Secret Service?"

"Yes, but we use the FBI offices sometimes and we are working with the FBI on this case."

"What case?"

"I don't want to upset you, but you may not be the first woman the General has attacked. The team did some investigating last night and there have been several disappearances that have occurred while he and his entourage are here negotiating. These have occurred over several months and only while he is here. All the disappearances that we have found so far have been hookers or street women, but the team is still investigating. There may be more. No one noticed the pattern until now. Now we think he may be running a slave ring and using his trips to the United States to find young girls and women to kidnap. We want to walk you through what happened and see if he said anything to you that may have given any clues to his intentions," he told her as he reached over and ran one hand up and down her thigh.

"Why me? Why did he pick me?" she wondered out loud.

"You're a beautiful woman, why wouldn't any man be crazy for you? I am." He tried to comfort her.

"You are? Really?" she asked with wonder in her voice. She had had her share of dates and never had any problems, but no one had ever called her beautiful or told her that they were crazy for her. She'd even been engaged a couple times, but something always happened and she thought she was just screwing it up. To have this amazing man say he was crazy about her made her heart melt.

"What are you doing?" she asked as he pulled the car over. They were nowhere near where they needed to be and she didn't think they had time for any stops.

"You're too far away, scoot over here," he said, patting the seat next to him.

She put her coffee in the holder and moved to where he indicated. Fastening the seat belt there, he slipped his hand into the V of her legs. "Perfect," he said and leaned down and kissed her

She melted into his arms and let him take her mouth, opening and giving him everything.

He was the most amazing kisser and lover. She had never been with anyone who could set her body afire the way he did. One look from him and she was gushing. Her panties would be wet all the time she was around him. Giggling to herself, she thought, when I'm allowed to wear panties. Remembering that she wasn't wearing underwear, she wiggled, wondering if he could feel the moisture through her jeans.

He broke the kiss and left her panting. With a quick squeeze between her legs, he pulled back onto the road. "We have to get going, it doesn't look good when the team leader is late. I should have been there already." He smiled at her and hit the gas.

"Oh, I'm sorry, did I make you late?" she asked, worried now. She hadn't realized he was the team leader, but it made sense. He was in control of everything. She smiled, remembering how he took control last night. Would she get to experience that again?

"Baby, we're fine. I'm always on time." He assured her with another squeeze between her legs.

If he kept that up, she would be coming before she got out of the truck.

Derek kept his hand where it was for the rest of the drive but didn't do anything more than hold her.

When they arrived, he pulled her out of his side of the SUV, sliding her down his body. Trapping her against the side of the truck, he ground his pelvis into hers. "See what you do to me? You'll be taking care of this as soon as we get out of here. I have plans for you and they are going to last all weekend." he growled in her ear, before placing a hard kiss on her lips and lowering her to the ground.

He grabbed her hand and pulled her into the building, her senses still swimming.

He strode straight through the lobby, not looking left or right, set on his goal to get this over so he could continue with his plans for Dottie. He knew this was going to take longer than he wanted it to. Hell, if he had his way they would have waited until Monday, but he knew it was best to get the debriefing over while things were fresh. If they waited, Dottie could forget a detail or decide it wasn't important enough to tell. This early, they could still do a forensic interview and have good results. The next few hours would not be comfortable for Dottie and he wouldn't be able to be with her, but she was strong and could do this.

Leading her to the conference room, he got her a cup of coffee and sat her down to explain how the next few hours would go and why he couldn't be with her.

As he finished up, the team started arriving. He quickly made introductions.

"Dottie, this hulk here is Tyler Thomas. He's a Secret Service agent and we've been on the same team for years." Tyler was shorter than Derek at six foot four, but just as bulky, with long blond hair which he wore in a braid down his back.

Tyler grabbed her hand and kissed the back of her knuckles. "If this big lug doesn't treat you right, you come see me, I'll take care of you," he said, mirth glimmering in his eyes.

Derek gave him a dirty look and introduced the remainder of the people at the table. Several were FBI agents and the other three were Secret Service.

After the introductions were made, Derek gave a quick briefing and one of the FBI agents and one Secret Service agent led her off to a private room for her interview.

They had her sit in the room and dimmed the lights. "Close your eyes," the female FBI agent, Tracy Smith, told her. With her eyes closed Dottie couldn't see the looks Tracy and the Secret Service agent, Dillon Polk, exchanged.

Tracy conducted the interview professionally and thoroughly. When she was sure Dottie had told her every detail and she seemed satisfied, Tracy gave her a big hug and they walked her back to the original room where Derek was waiting for her.

Standing as she entered the room, he quickly walked to her and pulled her into his arms. "I know that was tough, baby, are you good?"

Smiling, she nodded and leaned into him, wanting his strength. Even though it had only been a short time, she had come to depend on him.

Tracy looked at Derek and said, "Sir, Dillon and I are going to compare notes and will file our report by this evening."

Dismissing them with a nod, Derek's attention was all for Dottie. "Can you walk to the SUV, or do you need me to carry you?"

Smiling up at him, she answered, "I can walk, but can we go now? I really want a hot bath and a warm bed."

"Honey, I have both at my house and that's where you're going. Do you need to stop by your place and get anything, any medicine or stuff?"

"No, but some clean clothes would be nice," she answered.

"You won't need any clothes." He answered with a twinkle in his eye.

A shiver ran down her back and she gripped his hand tighter.

He followed he directions she gave to her condo and waited in the truck while she packed a small bag for the weekend, stating he needed to make some calls while he waited.

He pulled her to the middle of the truck and kept her close on the drive to his house. Before they got there, he drove through for food which they ate on the way, knowing that the donuts they had had were not enough. When they arrived, she was amazed. She had figured he lived in a condo or bachelor pad somewhere in downtown D. C., but no, he took her to a place on the edge of town. The neighborhood had sprawling ranches with room for horses. Each property had to be at least five acres and there were horses on almost all of them including the one he pulled up to.

Chapter Three

"Surprised? Yes, it's mine and the horses, too," he proudly stated, helping her out of the truck. Instead of taking her to the door, he took her around back to the fence. Whistling, he called the horses over. Patting one of them on the head, he told her, "This little filly is Patrice, and her partner here is Big Al. I've had them both for about ten years and we are all very happy. Aren't we, big boy?"

"Do you ride them?" Dottie asked, reaching up to pat Patrice.

"Yes, do you ride?" he asked, slipping one arm around her waist, and lifting her to reach the male horse.

"I haven't for years. I used to all the time before I moved away from home." She answered wistfully.

"Then that's something we will do together. One of my neighbors takes care of them while I'm on assignment. Later we'll go riding and I'll show you around the area. Right now, I have other plans for you." He was standing behind her and she could feel his erection against the middle of her back.

"Oh," she answered as he kissed the back of her neck and lifted her bride like, and carried her to the house.

The back door opened into a mudroom and he set her on the floor there. "Leave your things here and I'll meet you in the living room, straight through the kitchen." He planted a long, hard kiss on her and strode out of the room.

Things—what things was he talking about? She had left her briefcase and purse in the SUV and all she had was her clothes and shoes. Maybe he meant her shoes. He hadn't taken his off, but lots of people didn't wear shoes indoors. Slipping off her shoes and lining them up neatly by the door, she followed his directions and walked into the living room.

He was sitting on the couch and had a bottle of wine and two glasses on the coffee table in front of him.

Walking silently on the hardwood floors, he didn't appear to hear her until she stood in front of him. "Hi," she said shyly.

He looked up and it was difficult to read the expression on his face. "I thought I told you to leave your things in the mudroom."

"I left most of my stuff in the truck and all I had were my clothes and my shoes. I did leave my shoes."

"Why didn't you leave your clothes?"

"You wanted me to come in here...naked?" She shivered, not sure if she should be excited or scared.

"Obviously, you have a problem with that, can you tell me why?"

"I'm not used to going around without clothes. It's not something I'm comfortable with."

"Maybe you should practice while you are here. I want you naked," he practically growled.

"Oh," she said as she saw the lust fill his eyes. Could she do this? She just stood there looking at him.

"Dottie, take your clothes off or I'll tear them off." This time it was a growl.

"You, oh...okay." She stuttered, and slowly started removing her shirt and jeans.

When she was totally naked, she stood there not knowing what to do next. She wrapped her arms over her chest protectively and stood there looking at the floor.

"Come here, I want to look at you."

She walked over to stand between his wide-spread legs, wondering why he wanted to look at her. Didn't he see enough last night?

Standing there very self-consciously, she kept her arms crossed over her chest.

He gently took her arms and moved them to her sides. Looking up in her eyes, he smiled and she saw the kindness there. "Relax, I'm not going to do anything you don't want me to do." And he leaned up and took a nipple in his mouth. Sucking and licking the little nub, he moved his hands around and grabbed her buttocks, pulling her closer until they were as close as could be.

Standing up, he told her, "Wrap your legs around my waist."

He carried her into what she thought was his bedroom and the biggest bed she had ever seen.

"I had it custom made. There isn't another one like it," he said as he sat on the edge of the bed, her legs still wrapped around him. Holding her there, he continued to lick and suck on her breasts and nipples, taking as much of her soft flesh in his mouth as he could. "You taste so good, baby, have you ever come from someone playing with these?" he asked as he continued what he had been doing.

"No, but I think I'm going to." She answered panting.

"Yes, I think you're going to, too." He grinned as he started using his teeth and pulling her nipple, while he took one hand and started pinching and pulling the bud not in his mouth. "Come for me, baby, show me what you can do." He crooned as he bit her nipple harder and pinched harder.

She felt the wave starting and knew she was going over. Digging her fingers into his shoulders, she rubbed her clit up against him, that little bit of friction enough to send her over. Screaming his name, she crashed through her orgasm, letting wave after wave take her.

He held her tight through her completion and ran his hand up and down her back when she laid her head on his shoulder, panting. "I knew you could do it." He praised her as he lay back on the bed and turned them so that they were sprawled in the center.

Lying on his back, he pulled her to lie on top of him and held her until she was calm, whispering words of praise and encouragement.

When her breathing was back to normal, he lifted her and carried her into the biggest bathroom she had ever seen. Was everything this man did and have big? Sitting her on a stool, he started filling the huge tub. "You stay here, I'm going to get the wine," he instructed.

Leaving her sitting, he came back carrying the wine, a glass, a bucket of ice, and several condoms.

She looked at the condoms wide-eyed and smiled. Yep, a fun afternoon for Dottie.

By now the tub had filled and he quickly stripped, then picked her up and sat in the tub with her back to him, her legs inside of his.

Leaning back and pulling her with him, they sat for several minutes before he reached and poured a glass of wine. Holding it to her lips, he allowed her to drink before taking his own drink.

Setting the glass on a small table beside the tub, he turned her so that she was straddling his hips. He pulled her in for a deep kiss and reached for an ice cube. Rubbing the cube around her areola, her nipple instantly hardened. "Soon I will clamp these. Have you ever worn nipple clamps, Dottie?" he asked, running his tongue around the shell of her ear.

"Oh...oh," she moaned. She had been so tired when they left the FBI offices, she was sure she was going to sleep on the way to his house. Now sleep was the last thing on her mind. The difference in the sensations between the warm water and the ice was mind-blowing, and she couldn't believe her responses and her body's reactions. She had come more in the last few hours with Derek than she had with any other man. And to think, she hadn't thought he was interested in her.

Obviously, she was mistaken. If this wasn't interest, she didn't know what was. But could she be enough for him? She knew he was into BDSM but didn't know much about it. Time for an Internet search. It would be nice to have someone to talk to, but she didn't know anyone and definitely wasn't going to ask those questions to Derek.

Taking another piece of ice, he put it in his mouth and then took her nipple in his mouth, using his tongue to move the piece of ice around her nipple.

"Oh, God," she screamed. Adjusting herself on his lap, she felt his cock rub her folds and she started rubbing herself against him.

"Oh, you're just like a little kitten, rubbing your pussy against me. Baby, I'm not going to last long at this point." Pushing her bottom back toward his knees, he lifted her legs over his shoulder and pulled her core to his mouth. Taking another ice cube from the bucket, he slowly rubbed it through her folds, before pushing it inside her. "We need to cool this off." He grinned evilly and took another cube and pushed it inside her.

The cold in her core was something she had never experienced before and just when one cube melted and she thought she was going to get some relief, he put another one inside her.

Taking another cube, he slowly rimmed her puckered hole with it. She arched in his arms and screamed his name. "I have more tricks to show you, but first you are going to give me a little relief." Grabbing a condom, he donned it and pulled her to him, and fitted himself inside her, slowly pulling her down until he was fully inside her. He let her sit for a minute to adjust to him before he instructed, "hands on my shoulders, this is going to be rough and hard."

Grabbing her hips with both hands, he lifted her until he was poised just at her entrance. With a quick motion, he slammed her back down on him until he was buried as deep as he could go. He continued to do this, establishing a punishing rhythm until he couldn't hold back any longer.

"Hold on, Dottie, I'm going to come." He told her and he moved her up and down faster until she felt his release and found her own.

She collapsed onto his chest, panting. He wrapped his arms around her and held her tight to him. They lay in the warm water like that for several minutes.

He lifted her away from him. "Thank you, baby," he told her, looking into her deep into her ocean blue eyes and lifting her off of him.

She smiled and leaned in to cuddle with him. He held her for a minute, then lifted her and rose himself.

Disposing of the condom, he led her to the separate walk-in shower and started the water. Looking at her, he tapped his chin. "Have you ever shaved your pussy?" he asked, running his fingers over her curls.

"No," she answered, wondering where he was going with this.

"Would you let me do it?" he asked, grinning.

"Okay." She answered, not sure why she was agreeing, but seeing no reason to protest.

Sitting her on the bench in the shower, he turned to get what he would need. Setting his supplies on the bench next to her, he positioned her as he wanted her. Taking the shaving cream, he slathered it all over her mound and slipped a little on her clit.

"Oh, that's..." she moaned.

"Menthol, baby, interesting feeling isn't it?" he told her as he rubbed a little more into her folds and pushed a little into her asshole.

She arched off the bench and let out a little scream.

"Now you're going to have to hold still, so I don't accidentally nick your skin," he told her, stroking the razor over her.

Once he had her shaved, he grabbed the handheld showerhead and rinsed her, turning the setting to a forceful stream of water. He ran it up and down her folds, concentrating on her round hole and clit until she was squirming on the bench again.

"Tell me, have you ever used one of these to get yourself off?" he asked, aiming the spray at her clit.

"Oh God, yes," she answered, needing to 'get off' right now.

"Good answer, here's a reward," he said, pushing the spray closer to her clit and taking a finger and pushing it into her rear hole.

"Oh, I can't, stop it!" she screamed as she came for about the twentieth time in less than twenty-four hours.

Standing her up, he soaped and rinsed her all over before drying them both and carrying her to the bed. Laying her in the center, he crawled in with her and pulled a blanket over both of them.

"Sleep now, and when we wake, we'll have something to eat and more fun." He fitted her back to his front and possessively cupped a breast.

Once he was sure she was asleep, he grabbed a pair of sweatpants and went to check his messages. He wanted to see if the reports had been uploaded from the interviews and if there was any more information about the General.

He had a hard time concentrating on the reports. His mind kept drifting to Dottie and how perfect she was. He never let things distract him while he was working, but Dottie was going to be a big distraction.

Shaking his head to clear his thoughts, he turned back to the reports. Nothing he didn't expect to find. The interview with Dottie revealed nothing new. The General's staff was very uncooperative and the General himself claimed diplomatic immunity and refused to say anything more. How was he ever going to crack this case? Something was going to have to give. He didn't want any more women disappearing. He was sure the General or someone on his staff had something to do with it.

Pacing the room, he looked at the clock and saw Dottie had been sleeping for three hours while he had read all the reports and filed his own. Time for more fun. But first, he should feed her again. They had had a light lunch and the donut from this morning couldn't have filled her up and she needed her strength for what he had planned. There was still a lot of weekend left and he didn't need to report back in until Monday morning.

He quickly looked into the bedroom to make sure she was still okay. She had kicked off the blanket and was lying sprawled on the bed in all her glory. And what glory it was. Taking the sheet and covering her, he told his cock to wait and went to the kitchen to grill some steaks.

His kitchen was something he was proud of. He loved cooking and had everything a chef could want. Grabbing the steaks, he started heating the grill built into the stove. Grabbing a couple potatoes, he prepared them for roasting then went to his wine cellar in the basement for a bottle to go with the meal.

The main floor of the house was unassuming, but the basement was a playground. He had a state-of-the-art gym with every piece of equipment that was available. A wine cellar with over one thousand bottles of wine, several of which were very rare. And a dungeon. Even though he was part owner of The Mix, a very trendy BDSM club in town, he occasionally liked to bring a submissive home and play here. There had been very few women in his playroom and he planned on having one and only one there from now on. Little Miss Dottie Chapman was going to be introduced to this room very soon.

He grinned with the thought and ran up the stairs, eager to get to his woman.

When he walked into his kitchen, there she sat. Beautiful. Wearing one of his shirts and nothing else, she was what wet dreams were made of. He walked up to her and took her mouth in a kiss meant to let her know she was his and his alone. When he let her up for air, he gazed into her eyes and asked, "Hey beautiful, how are you? Did you sleep well? Are you hungry?" Then he slipped one hand down the open neck of her shirt, palming a nipple.

She shivered and smiled. "Best I've ever slept except for last night. What's on the menu? And don't answer me." She laughed.

"Oh...you're on the menu all right, my lovely. You're the main course. We'll have steaks first though." He growled at her and licked his lips.

Dottie felt a shiver run down her back and looked down at her hands, wondering what he had in mind. She knew little about the club that he owned other than it was a kink club. She had never been in that type of club and had no idea what went on in there. She wondered if she would find out.

While she had been thinking about his club, Derek must have asked her a question.

"Dottie, did you hear me?" he said to her.

"I'm sorry. I must not have been paying attention. What did you want?" she asked, smiling up at him.

"I asked how you wanted your steak and if you were good with roasted potatoes and a salad."

"Oh...It all sounds good. Medium-rare on the steak."

"Great, have a glass of wine, I just opened it and it's breathing in the chiller. Do you want to eat outside?"

"Outside sounds nice, let me go and put some clothes on," she answered him.

"You don't need anything more than what you're wearing. We'll be out back and no one can see us out there except the horses, and they don't care."

"I really don't feel comfortable just wearing one of your shirts," she argued.

"You'll be fine. If you get cold, I'll find a way to warm you. The food's ready, let's carry it out."

He reached down, and taking her hand, lifted her out of the chair. Handing her a plate of food, he grabbed her wineglass and one for himself, also carrying a plate and the bottle of wine. He led her out to the back and they sat at a very comfortable table. The chairs were nicely cushioned and huge. Thinking about Derek, everything about him was huge and it only made sense that his house would be made to fit him.

After they ate, he stood her up and started walking toward a glider on the porch, taking the wine and glasses with him.

"Shouldn't we take the plates in?" Dottie asked, a little nervous. What would he expect now?

"I'll get them later, come sit," he answered, pulling her over to the glider. He sat and pulled her down beside him.

He started the glider rocking and told her quietly, "If we don't make a lot of noise, we may see a deer or two. Usually, this time every evening they wander through here."

They sat in comfortable silence for several minutes. Dottie wasn't sure how long it was. It didn't take long before she relaxed into Derek, resting her head on his shoulder, and enjoying the rocking motion of the glider.

Derek slipped one arm around her shoulders and pulled her closer. He felt her shiver and asked, "Baby, are you cold? Do you want to go inside?"

Snuggling closer to him, she answered, "No, I'd like to give the deer a few more minutes." In truth, she was enjoying sitting close to Derek and wasn't ready to give up the intimacy.

She hadn't dated for several months and it had been more since she'd had sex. The sex she had with Derek over the last twenty-four hours was more than she'd had in the last ten years of her life. She had come more times than she had ever come before, and they were some of the best orgasms she had ever experienced. She had never had an orgasm like the ones Derek had given her, never.

Derek was one of the best-looking men Dottie had ever known. When she first met him, she almost melted when he spoke to her, and she was used to meeting lots of famous people in her work at the White House.

She had worked hard to get where she was. She had been one of the youngest reporters assigned to the White House and was very proud of what she had accomplished. The only thing missing in her life was a family. Because she traveled so much, she didn't even have a cat. Now maybe she could look toward a future. She wondered if Derek was interested in more than a weekend fling. The way he talked, it sure sounded like he was.

Derek sat, just enjoying the evening and being with Dottie. He didn't get to spend many evenings at home and even fewer with a beautiful woman. Dottie was perfect and would be even more so if she were submissive. He thought he saw a submissive streak in her, but she was such a strong woman, he wasn't sure she would be able to let him dominate her the way he needed to. He couldn't do it any other way. If he couldn't help her find her submissive side, he didn't know what he was going to do. The few times he had taken control with her, she had responded beautifully, and he wanted to experiment more with her.

He couldn't wait to get her in his dungeon. She would look beautiful strapped to a cross or bent over a spanking bench. Her breasts would be lovely with nipple clamps, and if things worked out between them, he would buy her jeweled clamps that she could wear for long periods of time. He thought about piercing her nipples but wanted to wait until after the babies were born.

He couldn't believe that he was thinking about having children. He had bought his home with a family in mind, but it hadn't happened in the last ten years, and he was getting to the age where he was ready to settle down. Hopefully, Dottie would want to do this with him.

While they were both sitting there thinking about the future, a small family of deer appeared. Dottie clasped his hand tightly and covered her mouth to keep silent. They sat quietly and watched the deer for several minutes and Dottie almost squealed with glee when she saw one of the deer walk up to the horses. Patrice nuzzled the deer and after a few minutes, it hopped away, the other deer following.

"That was amazing, do they come every night?" she asked, her voice filled with wonder.

"I'm not here often, but every time I've been home, they are here. I have them all named. The one that walked up to Patrice is Ralph, and every time he comes, he goes to see her. I think he has a thing for her."

Dottie giggled and said, "I wonder if that would work and what the offspring would look like."

"I'm not sure, but I think Ralph and Patrice would like to find out," Derek responded.

They sat for a few more minutes before Derek stood, pulling Dottie with him. He handed her the wine and grabbed the plates off the table. Leading her into the kitchen, he sat her on a barstool and poured her a glass of wine. He quickly and efficiently cleaned the kitchen while Dottie sat and watched, sipping her wine.

Chapter Four

He walked over to her and took her now empty wineglass, rinsing it and putting it in the dishwasher with the other glasses. Taking her hand, he led her to the couch in the living room and sat, pulling her onto his lap.

He took her mouth with his and probed deeply, not letting her go for several minutes. When he released her, they were both panting and aroused. "Dottie, I want to ask you some questions."

"Okay," she answered, wondering what he was going to ask.

"Honey, don't worry, it's not bad. I just want to know if you know anything about me and what I like to do, what I need to do."

"I know you opened The Mix and are part-owner, but I'm not really sure what goes on there. I've never been, and I don't know anyone who has except you."

"Okay, The Mix is a BDSM club. Do you know what that means?" he answered as he rubbed her back

"Not really. I know what it stands for Bondage Domination Submission and Masochism, but I'm not sure what all that means."

"Do you want me to explain it to you?" he asked, slipping his hand under her shirt, and rubbing his hand over her bare back.

"I guess if it's important to you," she answered, not sure she wanted to get into this. She really had no idea what she was getting into. Could she do this for Derek? Would he want her if she couldn't?

"Okay, in order: bondage, the art of restraining someone, either bodily—like I did you last night, by having you hold your hands on my shoulders—or with scarves, ropes, or other tools. Any questions?"

Dottie shook her head no. *Tie me up? I don't think so.* Not after what had happened in the General's room, but the more she thought about Derek doing it, the more she tingled and her pussy leaked. What would it be like to be helpless under his control? The small tastes he had given her had whetted her appetite. Maybe she could do this.

"Next, submission. Giving up control to someone else. There are several degrees of this. Some people give up all control in what is called a TPE or Total Power Exchange. In a TPE, the dominant, or me, would take total control of you, the submissive. I would control everything—all your daily activities, everything in the bedroom. I would take over your life." Seeing the shocked expression on Dottie's face, he leaned down and kissed her.

"Don't worry, I don't want that. It's a lot of responsibility and I want a woman with some fight in her. What interests me is control in the bedroom and any time we make love. I need to control all sexual situations. I need to be in charge and determine how everything will play out. I said the bedroom, but if I were to take you here on the couch, and it will happen, I would be in control." As he had been talking, he slowly moved her hands around to her back and was holding both of her wrists in one hand. With his other hand, he unfastened the buttons on the shirt she was wearing and slipped it off her shoulders, baring her breasts to him.

Leaning down, he took a nipple between his teeth and slowly tugged. "I need this. I need to know you will try this with me. Are you willing to explore this with me? I know you're a strong, independent woman and I don't want you to give any of that up, but I want to control you when we are making love and playing sexually, will you let me do that? Try it with me, baby." Even as he talked, he continued his assault on her breasts, licking, nipping, and tugging on them with his mouth and free hand. Dottie couldn't think. The way he explained it made it seem so simple. Be herself when she was at work and give into him when they were together. Was it that simple?

"Derek, stop a minute. I want to make sure I understand what you are asking. You want me to give you control when we're together and be myself the rest of the time?"

"Baby, that's pretty simple, but basically it. I don't have to control you all the time even when we're together, but anytime we are alone and playing, I will be in control."

As he said the last, the hand that had been playing with her breasts dove between her legs and ended all conversation. Standing up and lifting her with him, he growled in her ear. "Wrap your legs around me."

When she did, he walked up to the wall and slid down his sweats, "Is it safe? Do I need protection or are you on something?"

This was the first time he had asked. All of the other times he had taken her, he had used protection. What was different now?

"Yes, I'm on the pill and I just had a physical and I'm all clear." She answered against his skin, kissing, licking, and nipping wherever she could reach.

He fitted himself to her and drove home. Bracing her against the wall, her hands were now trapped behind her back and she depended on him for her total support. If he were to move, she would fall.

He cupped her buttocks in both hands and started a fast and furious pace. "This isn't going to take long. I've been hot for you since before we ate," he said, not slowing his down.

He had set a hard and pounding rate. It felt like he was driving her into the wall. All she could do with her hands trapped behind her was to lean into him and go for the ride, and what a ride it was.

It didn't take long before she felt his release filling her. She had never realized the difference a condom made. Always before she had insisted on them. No accidents for Ms. Dottie Chapman, but with Derek something was different. It was true she was on the pill and chances were very slim, but if by some small miracle she should become pregnant, it wouldn't be bad. Then she would have a piece of Derek for her very own, and it didn't matter if he were willing to participate or not. Just the thought of a little Derek running around messing up her life brought light to her soul. It was too early to talk to Derek about children, but she wondered if he wanted them. She hadn't before, but now it wouldn't be so bad.

She came out of her musing to see Derek staring at her. "You okay? Did I hurt you?" he asked as he pulled her away from the wall and gently stood her on her feet. After making sure she was steady, he started rubbing her hands and arms, restoring circulation, and making sure he hadn't hurt her.

"I'm fine. That was something else, are you okay?" She leaned into him and slowly brought her arms around his neck, wincing a little at the stiffness in them. Even though he had rubbed them, they were still a little sore.

"A hot shower will loosen those muscles. Up for some water play?" He grinned as he adjusted his sweats and threw her over his shoulder.

Giggling (she never giggled) and screeching, she grabbed him around the waist and bit his back. "Does that answer your question, big boy?" She half-laughed, half-growled.

"You are so going to pay. I owe you a spanking for earlier anyway. I know we haven't talked about punishments, but we will very soon, and you have earned yourself several in the past few hours. It may be time to pay up."

"Punishment? What punishment?" she asked as he continued down the hall, bouncing her on his shoulder as he went. Spanking? He was going to spank her? Was that part of his kink? Did he like to beat women up? Was there a difference between being beaten and a spanking? Never one to be shy, she asked him, "Derek, are you telling me you like to beat women?" Stopping abruptly, he flipped her to her feet and grabbed her chin.

"Let's get one thing straight right now. *I. Never. Beat. Women. Never!* I will never hit you in anger, and I only administer erotic punishments, not beatings. A beating is a brutal act by someone who has no respect for women. I would *never* hit a woman in anger, and if that's what you think this is about you really have no idea what I'm into." Taking a deep breath to calm himself, he loosened his hold on her chin and gently placed a hand on each of her shoulders.

Squatting slightly so that he was face-level with her, he looked in her eyes and told her, "Dottie, I didn't mean to sound harsh. I would never hurt you in anger. The punishments I give you may sting and you may be sore for a day or two, but nothing, ever, in anger. Baby, my main goal is to take care of you. I treasure this body of yours and if you submit to me, I will care for it as my own. I treasure you and don't ever want to see you hurt. I know after what happened to you last night this must all be confusing, but please, bear with me and let me teach you how to be submissive to me. I know I haven't explained this to you yet, but you, as the submissive, hold all the control. When we start to play, I will give you a word, a safe word. It will be something you wouldn't normally say and when you use that word, everything stops and we talk. When we play, you will have all the power to stop everything. Any time it gets to be too much or you get scared or for any other good reason, you say the word, and everything stops. You have the control to stop everything at any time. It's actually the submissive who holds all the power in the relationship. You control how far things go, and if it goes too far for you, we stop. We haven't talked about limits and what kind of things you want to explore if you want to do this with me, but we will." As they were talking, he was slowly walking her toward the bedroom. "For tonight, all I want to do is flip you over my lap and spank that little ass bright pink. I'm not going to give you a safe word tonight, you won't need it. If you tell me to stop I will, but I don't think you will tell me to. Are you willing to try for me, Dottie?" By now he had her in the bedroom and he was sitting on the bed with her standing in front of him between his legs. Dottie looked at him and considered everything he had said. If what he said was true, she could stop everything, any time. If she had the power to stop and set limits, what would it hurt to try? If he wanted to do something she didn't, she could say no. Better make sure. "Derek, let me make sure I understand.

I set the limits, I can stop whatever we're doing with a word, and if I don't want to do something I don't have to?" Could it really be that simple?

"That's pretty much right but I will push your limits. I want you to explore and try different things. Some of the things I ask you to try you may not be comfortable with, but I will want you to try them for me. Are you willing to agree to that?" As he said this, he had pulled her closer and was running his hand up and down her bare back.

Dottie looked down and she was naked. When had that happened? Thinking again about what he said, she answered, "What kind of things do you want me to try?"

"We will talk more about that later, for tonight I want to spank you and put a pair of clamps on those lovely nipples." Reaching in the bedside drawer, he pulled out a pair of what looked like earrings.

"They look like earrings," she observed.

He showed her how the worked, then leaned down and took one nipple in his mouth. Licking and sucking the small nub, he continued until her nipple was firm and distended. He quickly applied the clamp, careful not to make it too tight.

"Oh, that feels... I can feel it all the way down to my...oh." She finally got out and started to do a little dance.

Smiling up at her, Derek quickly took her other nipple in his mouth, applying the same treatment. While he was applying the second clamp, he flicked the first with his fingers.

Dottie didn't know what was happening, but her pussy was gushing and her breasts felt full and very sensitive. Moaning, she leaned into Derek.

"Now I'm going to turn you over my lap and spank you. This first spanking will be for not leaving your clothes in the mudroom like I told you to. We'll start with ten because it's your first offense. There will be times I ask you to count the swats, but not today. If it gets to be too much, I will stop, but I think you can take this."

As he was talking to her, he pulled her so that she was lying over his lap. She braced her hands on the floor for balance, and her toes barely touched.

"I'll let you brace yourself this first time, but in the future, I will bind your hands behind your back and I will be in total control of you."

Dottie shuddered and her pussy gushed even more. Who knew something like this would turn her on? Maybe she did want to explore more with Derek.

He started rubbing his hand in slow circles over her lower back and buttocks, slipping his fingers into her crack and rimming her asshole. "This little hole will be mine. Soon," he murmured, and pulling his hand back, smacked her right cheek.

"Oh." She grunted. She hadn't been expecting it, and the shock of it startled her.

After the smack, he went back to rubbing, slipping his fingers in her slit and stroking her clit. After a few seconds of stroking and rubbing, he applied another smack, making her jerk again.

Every time he smacked, she jerked and her breasts jiggled, moving the clamps and causing her pussy to gush more.

He continued in that way, smacking, and rubbing until all ten smacks were done. Flipping her over, he cuddled her in his lap, one hand flicking the clamps on her breasts. "Oh God, Derek, what are you doing to me? I need to come so bad, please." She moaned against his chest where he was holding her.

"Are you okay? Did you like that?" he asked her, slipping one hand down to her slit and slowly rubbing her clit.

Arching in his lap, she moaned again and looked pleadingly into his eyes. "Please, Derek, you have to make me come."

Continuing to play with her clit, he smiled an evil smile. "Dottie, orgasm denial is another form of punishment. I can keep you on the edge for hours and not give you what you need."

"Huh? Denial, what...why would you do that?" Dottie was sure she hadn't heard him right.

"Baby, that's just another punishment, or I could make you come so many times that you screamed for mercy," he told her, upping the pressure and speed on her clit.

She was now arching and writhing on his lap and really needed relief. "There's no way you could make me come so many times I screamed, but I'd take once right now."

"Baby, it's called 'orgasm torture' and I can and will do it. That sounded almost like a dare, are you daring a Dom?"

Needing to come so bad she didn't care, she grabbed his wrist and tried to get him to speed up or press harder or something. She answered. "If you're so big and bad, then do it, Mister."

"Oh baby, you are so in for it, but first—" he quickly flipped her onto her back in the middle of the bed and was crouching over her. Using one hand, he flicked the clamps on her nipples, moving back and forth between them, and applied more pressure and speed on her clit with the other. Even though he was applying more pressure, it still wasn't enough.

"Oh please, don't torture me, please," she pleaded. She was arching off the bed and pleading for him to end the torment. He kept it up, keeping her writhing and pleading for what seemed like an hour, but was only a few minutes.

When he finally let her come, she felt like she was levitating off the bed. Her whole body was suspended in space and her limbs were no longer attached. If he kept giving her orgasms like this, she would never leave. She would be his slave forever and do anything he asked.

When she finally found the power of speech again, she looked at him and asked, "How do you do that? Each one is better than the last and they are all better than anything I ever experienced before. You've ruined me for any other man. After you, no one will ever match up."

"Exactly, there will be no one after me. If another man even thinks about looking at you, I will knock him off his feet. And you had better not think of looking at another man or your ass will be so red and hot that you won't sit for a month and you won't come for a month either. Do. You. Understand?"

Wow, not possessive at all, but somehow she loved it. Smiling, she nodded, unable to form words.

He leaned down and took her in a branding kiss, marking her as his. "Don't forget it either."

Now for the other side of the spectrum, he thought, he had just shown her what orgasm denial was like, time to show her what a few forced orgasms were like. Dottie had dared him and he never resisted a dare. Never.

"Okay, you issued a dare earlier. Now for a few forced orgasms. Before we start, I need to prepare a few things and I am going to restrain you. You lie here and rest. I will be right back." He planted a quick kiss on her already throbbing lips and tweaked the nipple clamps.

Leaving, he left her lying on the bed to contemplate what he had said while he quickly ran down to the playroom to get a few toys and some soft scarves. They really should have been doing this down there, but he didn't want to take her there yet. He had planned to, but he didn't feel she was ready. Depending on how well she took what he had planned next, maybe they could play there tomorrow afternoon. The next day was Monday and back to reality. He didn't know if she would give him more than the one weekend or not, but he was going to try for more.

He knew he would see her again. He couldn't avoid her. Between what had happened with the General and his work, he would be seeing her all the time. If he were lucky, maybe he could get himself assigned to protect her. That would be perfect. If he could do that, then he would have an excuse to be with her 24/7 and she would have to put up with him.

Grabbing what he wanted from the toy room, he sprinted back up the stairs. When he got to his room, the bed was empty. What the hell? He hadn't been gone more than two minutes.

Looking in the bathroom, he found her sitting on the toilet crying, the nipple clamps in her hands.

"What are you doing? I thought I told you to stay still." He asked, taking the clamps from her.

"I needed to come in here, and then those were hurting so I took them off. Why didn't you tell me how bad they hurt coming off?" she asked accusingly.

"Honey, you weren't supposed to take them off without me. How was I to know you would do that? Here, let me see if I can help." And he leaned down to take one of her poor nipples in his mouth.

She quickly covered each breast with a hand and said, "No! Don't touch me!" and immediately started sobbing.

Grabbing her in his arms, Derek picked her up and carried her to the bed.

Sitting with her on his lap, he held her tight and let her cry for a while. It had been an emotional time for her, and Derek knew she needed to let it all out.

Sometimes he could be an ass and think only of himself. He had put aside everything she had been through and let his dick do the thinking. He hadn't even considered that she had no idea what she was getting into and just kept pushing and pushing. No wonder she was sobbing in his arms.

Lying back on the bed, he stretched her out on top of him and pulled a light blanket over both of them.

Holding her, he let her cry until she had it out of her system. Eventually she stopped crying and fell into a deep sleep.

Derek lay awake most of the night, keeping her on top of him, wanting her close. Sometime in the early hours of the morning, he finally drifted off to sleep.

Chapter Five

When Derek woke, it was to a beautiful sight. Dottie was straddling him and had bent to lick and suck the skin on his chest and abs. Swirling her tongue over and over his skin and rubbing her little pussy over his manhood. What a way to wake up. He lay for several minutes and let her do her thing before she lifted and saw him watching her.

"Morning lover," she said in a deep, sexy voice.

"Morning yourself," he replied, pulling her to him for a deep soul-reaching kiss. "You may continue." He sounded like a sultan granting his slave permission to serve him.

"Oh I may, may I?" she said saucily.

Fisting his hand in her hair, he pulled her over him until her breasts were dangling over his mouth like ripe peaches waiting to be plucked. Which, of course, he did. Taking a nipple between his teeth, he pulled, stretching her dangling fruit until she made a little squeal. Releasing her nipple and her hair, he cupped the back of her head and grinned. "You may."

Not saying a word, she went back to her task.

He folded his arms under his head and lay back to watch the show.

Dottie licked and sucked her way over his chest, taking each nipple briefly between her teeth, and worked her way down to his navel, where she swirled her tongue around, briefly dipping in before following the trail of hair to his treasure.

Scooting back toward his knees, she took him in her hand and looked up into his face for permission. "Anything you want."

She smiled before leaning down to run her tongue from the base to the head of his cock. Wrapping both hands around him, she licked the small white droplet of moisture there, before taking as much as she could in her mouth. Smiling when Derek groaned, she pulled back, lightly scraping her teeth against him.

When he shifted his hips and fisted both hands in her hair, she did it again and again, loving the feel of power she had over this dominant man.

Taking as much of him in her mouth as she could, she hollowed her cheeks and licked and sucked him until, using his hands in her hair, he took control of her head and started fucking her face.

"I'm going to come. I hope you swallow. If not, you need to pull back now," he groaned and eased up the grip on her hair.

When after a few seconds she didn't move, he held her head tight and let himself go, ramming his dick in her mouth faster and faster and hitting the back of her throat with each stroke until his release. Letting go of her hair, he cupped the back of her head and held her to him, panting and trying to catch his breath.

Dottie cleaned him off with her tongue and released him from her mouth. Laying her head on his thigh, she grinned with satisfaction. She had brought this man to his knees. She had taken the power and done this to him. He may be the dominant, but she held the power, and it felt good.

She lay there, her head on his thigh for several minutes until she felt him relax and his breath calm, then she crawled up his body, making sure to drag herself against him until she could lay her head on his shoulder, running her hand over the skin she had licked earlier.

Looking up into his smiling face, she asked, "Was it okay, lover?" Her voice was deep and gravelly and full of satisfaction and confidence.

"Better than okay, and don't get over-confident, I allowed you to do that."

"Yes, lover," she answered him, like she knew better.

"You had better watch it, girl, or I'll make good on the dare that was put down last night and show you just how I control that body" his voice rumbled with sexual tension and he pulled her up to take her lips with his.

When he broke off the kiss, her eyes were wide and her pussy gushed more. With one kiss, one look, one word, this man had total control over her, mind, and body. Everything and everyone else was forgotten. How could he do that to her? If she stayed with him, she was going to have to build a resistance to him or he would get his way all the time. She couldn't have that.

But that was exactly what he wanted. Total control over her mind and body all the time. Could she give it to him? Was she willing to be what he wanted? He had talked about tying her up and beating her, but that's not what he called it, restraints, and punishments, was there a difference? Did the difference matter? She knew if she stayed with him long enough, he would want to take her to his club. What kind of things happened there? What would he want to do to her?

How was she going to get all her questions answered? She couldn't ask him and didn't dare say anything about him beating her. He really went off the deep end when she had accused him of that last night. She wasn't going there again.

This weekend had been fun, but she would be glad to go home tonight and have some time to think. She really needed it. Even though she had loved every minute with Derek up to her meltdown last night, she needed some time.

Derek saw the confusion in her eyes and wondered how it would affect them. Feeling the need to distract her from her thoughts, he sat up and grabbed her under the arms, and pulled her to straddle his hips again. Leaning down, he took her in another bruising kiss.

"Food, then I think we'll go for a ride. This afternoon, we will play," he told her with a big smile on his face as he pointed her toward the shower. "You shower in here. I'm going to grab a quick shower in the guest room and then I'll start breakfast. Get dressed, and when you come out, we'll eat and then go. I know the horses are ready for some exercise, and so am I." Slapping her on her bare ass, he pointed her to the shower.

The slap on her ass reminded her of last night. What he had done was definitely not beating. She didn't know what to call it. Maybe that was what he had been trying to tell her. The difference between what had happened and what she had thought was going to happen was huge. Last night had been the most erotic night of her life before she took those stupid clamps off. And that really wasn't his fault, but he could have warned her.

She wondered what had just happened. She had hoped they would play all day. Disappointed, Dottie took her first shower alone in two days. She never realized how lonely a shower could be. Hurrying through what she needed to do, she returned to the bedroom, a towel loosely wrapped around her, hoping Derek would be there and she could accidentally drop the towel and get him to play. Finding the room empty, she walked down the hall to the kitchen, still in the towel.

Derek was standing with his back to her, cooking. Walking up to him, she dropped the towel and wrapped her arms around him from behind. "Hey, lover," she said in his ear, her voice low and gravely.

Turning, he wrapped his arms around her and grabbed both her buttocks. "I thought I told you to get dressed. I will add that to the list of transgressions for this afternoon. Does my baby need a little relief this morning before we go for our ride?" he asked, nibbling on her neck as he lifted her onto the island in the middle of the room.

Pulling her legs wide open and her bottom to the very edge of the surface, he leaned down and took her clit in his mouth. Licking, sucking, and nipping the little bud, he brought her right to the edge. When she didn't think she could take any more, he pulled back and stood her up.

"Go get dressed now. And no more topping from the bottom. If you're good for the rest of the morning, I'll tell you what that means later and then I'll let you come later." He grinned wickedly and sent her off with a pinch and twist to her right nipple.

Muttering to herself, Dottie stomped down the hall. She knew what to do about this. If he didn't want to take care of her, she had been single for a long time. She could handle this on her own.

"Oh, and Dottie, if you make yourself come, you won't come at my hand for the rest of the week! And that's a promise!"

Dottie continued stomping down the hall. How the fuck would he know anyway?

"Dottie, I will know and I don't threaten, I promise." He was laughing...laughing at her.

Dottie slammed the door to the bedroom so hard it rattled the pictures on his dresser. Throwing herself on the bed, she reached between her legs. How would he know? But she knew somehow, he would. Grabbing her clothes, she quickly got dressed and sat on the side of the bed for a few minutes, trying to calm herself down.

After a few minutes, Derek walked into the room with her shoes. "Here, baby, let's eat and go riding, then I promise I will take care of all your needs. Be a good girl for me."

Who could resist the puppy dog look in his eyes? Smiling, she put her shoes on and allowed him to lead her to the kitchen to eat.

After they consumed an enormous amount of food, he led her to the stables and they saddled the horses. They rode around his property, then he took her to a designated riding area and they rode there for over an hour, meeting several people also exercising their horses.

"During the week, it's not as crowded, but everyone comes out on Saturday and Sunday," he told her.

Walking the horses slowly to cool them down after their ride, Derek told her of his life.

"I was kind of a rebel in school, bigger than anybody there and meaner. More than my mom could handle and I constantly frustrated my dad, who was as big as I am. Finally, somehow I managed to graduate and dad had had it with me. He gave me two choices, go out or my own or join the service. He didn't care which branch, he just wanted me to have some discipline. So...I joined the Marines. Best decision of my life. I met some great people and made some lifelong friends. Several of which you were introduced to yesterday," he told her.

"Tyler, Link, and I were all in the same unit. We found Dillon and Trent when we joined the Secret Service. We've all been part of the same team for several years and are closer than a lot of brothers. We all have each other's backs."

He went on to tell her about his family. "I have three sisters, one older and two younger. I think that's part of the reason I was such a rebel. Too much estrogen in one house. Dad and I never had a chance. I'm not as close with my family as I would like to be, but once I retire, I plan on mending that. Enough about me, tell me about yourself." He grabbed her hand as they slowly walked the horses.

"My story's pretty boring. I was the good girl, honor roll all through high school and college. I went to college on a full scholarship, I'm an only child, my mom and dad are both gone. I have an aunt and uncle still living, but I'm not sure where they are. I've been pretty much on my own for a long time. I moved away from home when I started college. My mom and dad wanted me to stay home and marry a boy that I had been dating. He was from a good family and it would have been a good match, but it wasn't what I wanted. Mom and Dad never got over their disappointment in me. They were killed in a car wreck while I was at college. The funeral was small and that was the last time I was home. They left everything to a distant cousin. I got nothing."

He could tell by her voice that she was still a little bitter. "Baby, I'm sorry you went through that, but I'm sure that if they could see you now, they would be proud of who you are and what you've become."

"I hope so," she said.

Chapter Six

They rode the rest of the way back to his stable in silence, both thinking different things.

Derek was planning the afternoon, even though they had had a huge breakfast a few hours ago. He was going to feed her again and then they were going to spend some quality time in the playroom.

He knew Dottie had some reservations about the lifestyle and that this was a big step, but he felt that she was ready. He wanted to finish what he had started last night. She had dared him, and he never...never passed up a dare. He couldn't wait to see her face after her fourth or fifth forced orgasm. He wondered how many he could get out of her before she gave in.

Dottie was thinking about her life and how different it would have been if she had done what her parents wanted her to do. The boy they had wanted her to marry wasn't that bad, he just wasn't someone she was interested in. She had dated him several times and they even "went steady" while she was in school.

But she wanted more out of her life. She wanted to see beyond her small town. She wanted to travel. Her parents had never understood her need to go out and see the world. They were content to stay in their little box and not venture forth.

"It's too dangerous for a girl all on her own," they told her. "You'll never make it and you'll come crawling back to us, crying," her father said.

The boy she had been dating had looked sadly at her when she told him she was going away to college, but he understood and they had remained friends for several years after she left. The few times she had gone home, he was always there to see her and they still had fun together.

While Dottie and Derek had been lost in their thought, the horses had taken them home. Coming out of their collective thoughts, they realized they were not only home, but still holding hands.

Derek slipped off his horse first, then helped Dottie down, sliding her against his body all the way. "Let's rub the horses down, and then I'll find us some lunch. Then we play," he told her, pulling her to her toes for a kiss.

* * * *

After they finished eating, Derek took her hand and started to lead her to his dungeon. "Derek, I'd really like a shower before we..." She left the thought open.

"Honey, I'll take care of all of that, just follow me," he said, not letting go of her hand and pulling her along behind him.

Trust, this was all about trust and Dottie knew whatever Derek had planned, it would be fun. Following him down the stairs, she felt the trepidation build. Could she do this? Was she really going to let him tie her up and beat her? She really had to stop thinking of it that way. It was punishment and restraint. *Totally different from tying up and beating,* she tried to tell her brain. Somehow, she didn't think she'd ever be able to make the distinction.

Safe words. She needed to ask Derek before anything happened, what her safe word was, and she needed to remember that she could stop everything with that word. She had the control. She said when she needed to stop. Would he really stop if she used a safe word? How would she find out without trying it? She had so many questions and no one to ask. What had she gotten herself into?

They were now standing in front of a door in his basement. She assumed it was to his dungeon. Derek was looking at her like he had just said something she needed to respond to. Smiling, she looked at him innocently.

"I don't know what's going on in that pretty little head of yours, but you need to come back to me. Your focus for the afternoon is me and me only, got it?"

She smiled and nodded again. No way she was telling him what she had been thinking about.

"Dottie, I asked you to strip, let's get going." He stood towering over her, his hand crossed over his chest, every bit the impatient male.

Trepidation still building, Dottie quickly removed her clothes and stood there, not sure what to do next.

Derek keyed a code in the pad next to the door and led her into the semi-dark room. Looking around, it was hard to see the walls and corners of the room, the only light being in the middle, the rest of the room in shadows.

Dottie strained her eyes, trying to see what was hiding. Wondering what was in the room and what he was going to do to her.

Taking her by the hand, he led her to a normal-looking sofa, and sitting down, pulled her into his lap. "Relax, nothing's going to jump out at you. There's nothing hiding in the corners." He pulled a remote out of his pocket and slowly turned the lights up until the entire room was lit.

Standing, with her held close to him, he walked her to the wall directly in front of them. "This wall is where I will restrain you. See the hooks and eyes for the restraints?" he said, showing her the various heights at which they had been placed. "I can restrain you in a variety of positions, using a variety of restraints."

Taking her hand, he pulled her further down the wall. "These are the things that I could use to restrain you," he said, showing her various scarves, ropes, belts, cuffs, and chains. "Feel them and notice how different each one feels against your skin." He showed her how the leather cuffs were lined with fur and that the chains attached to them so that they did not touch her skin.

Taking four of the leather cuffs and carrying them with him, he walked her further into the room to the back wall. "This is a St. Andrew's Cross. This is where we will play today." As she looked at the cross, he knelt down behind her and fastened one set of the leather cuffs to her ankles.

Turning her to face him, he slowly backed her up to the cross. "For our first session of play, I will have you facing me and I won't blindfold you. We'll save that for later," he said as he knelt down to fasten her legs to the cross, gently spreading them wide.

Once he had her legs positioned where he wanted them, he took the other set of cuffs and fastened them around her wrists. Then he put a belt around her waist so she couldn't arch away from the cross and fastened her wrists to her waist belt so that her arms were straight at her sides. He had seen women restrained with their arms above their head, but he frequently liked to keep the arms at the side. It wasn't as tiring for the woman and her shoulders didn't get sore. There were some situations where the arms above the head were beneficial, but it wasn't always necessary, and with the arms down, he could play longer without worrying about unnecessary pain or stiffness.

"Now, I believe a dare was issued last night. If I remember correctly, there was something about me forcing orgasms and the number of times I could make you come. I think we'll start with five and increase if from there if we need to."

"Oh, God, you wouldn't." Dottie didn't know what a forced orgasm was, and she wasn't sure she wanted to find out.

"Yes, I would," he said with a wicked grin.

Turning his back, Derek walked over to a cabinet built into the wall and started rummaging through it, humming. It sounded like he was humming the Police song "Every Breath You Take."

Dottie didn't know whether she should be scared or not. She had never even heard of "forced orgasms" and had no idea what he was going to do to her. Was it even possible to force an orgasm?

She had always had so much trouble achieving that goal before Derek that she had no idea what to expect. She did know that she had had more orgasms since meeting Derek than she had in the last ten years. Maybe this wasn't going to be so bad after all.

Derek had never hurt her and had always been kind and considerate. Why should she expect anything different? Finally having the matter settled in her mind, Dottie relaxed, anxious to see what he would do.

When he turned back to her, his hands were empty except for a soft white rope. "First I'm going to tie your breasts. Not too tight, but I do want to see them bound."

Taking the rope in his hands, he started to slowly wind it around the base of her right breast. After he had wrapped the rope around several times, he moved to the left breast and gave it the same treatment. Once he had both breasts wrapped, he pulled the rope to her back and let it trail down. "We may have use for that later," he said as he pulled a pair of nipple clamps out of his pocket.

"Oh, Derek…I don't know, they hurt so bad…do I have to?" She whined.

"I'll make it good for you. I'd really like you to try for me. I want to show you the difference between what you did last night and how I would have removed them," he told her as he leaned down to take a nipple in his mouth. While he was sucking her nipple, he reached down and fingered her clit.

"Ooh, yes, I'll do whatever you want." She moaned, unable to control herself.

Slipping one finger inside her, he pressed against a spot she didn't even know she had and she screamed his name.

"That's one," he said smugly.

He applied the clamps quickly and then pulled something out of his pocket.

"This is a butterfly vibrator. It clamps on your clit, and when I click this remote it vibrates." He told her and proceeded to attach the clamp and start it.

Then he pulled a long, thin stick-like object out of his pocket. "This is an anal vibrator. It's slim and shouldn't hurt going in." He told her as he applied lube liberally to the object, then leaning down, started lubing her rear hole pressing his finger in and out going a little further each time. When he had her relaxed and she'd quit tensing he slid the vibe inside her, he started it.

Once he had her clit and ass humming, he pulled a huge dildo out of his vest.

"You are not putting that in me," Dottie said, her eyes wide. How many pockets did the man have anyway, and where was all this stuff coming from?

"Yes, I am. Where it goes is up to you." He snickered.

"Where, what?" Where could he put that? The obvious place was her pussy, but he didn't mean to put that monster up her bottom. Oh hell no. It would never fit.

"It will never fit," she echoed out loud.

"Yes, it will, it's smaller than I am, and I plan on taking that ass and soon."

"You want to...you know...me there?" No one had ever wanted to take her there. Derek had been hinting at that all weekend, but she hadn't taken him seriously.

"Yes, I will. This will help you get ready to take me. It will help you stretch. Before we get to that point I have some smaller plugs you'll wear a few hours each day. I'll work you up to this and me. But first I have a dare to complete."

Dottie couldn't stop staring at the dildo he had. It was much larger than what he had in her now and the vibe felt big enough.

He leaned down and took her mouth in a scorching kiss, focusing all her attention on him and her body. Taking both hands, he cupped her now red and swollen breasts, flicking the clamps on her nipples.

"I think it's time to take the ropes off for now. We may play more with them later." Derek knew this was the first time she had had her breasts bound and he didn't want to leave the ropes on too long.

As he slowly removed the ropes rubbing and stroking her skin as it was revealed, he upped the speed on both vibes and made sure to flick the clamps on her nipples as he went along.

By the time he had her breasts unbound, Dottie was ready to come again. Staring into her eyes, he upped the speed on the butterfly and pinched a nipple clamp, hard.

Dottie screamed and came, shaking on the cross. "Oh, my God, not again." She screamed.

"And again," Derek said, as he pulled both nipple clamps off at once and she continued screaming and coming.

Dottie had just come three times in rapid succession. Spent, she slumped on the cross, panting.

"That was three, I believe I promised two more," he told her, walking away from her.

Oh, God, what is he getting to torture me with now? I don't think I can take two more. I'll pass out first. Dottie's mouth was dry and her face was dripping sweat. Now she knew what a forced orgasm was. She wasn't sure she liked it. Maybe that was why it was called punishment.

Derek walked back up to her with a water bottle and wet cloth. Taking the cloth, he wiped her face and chest before giving her some of the water to drink.

"Better?" he asked her.

Nodding, she smiled. He did care enough to take care of her. Even though she was new to this kind of play, she knew that Derek was special and not all men treated their women like he did.

He apparently was giving her a little break and she was glad of it. Her body and her mind both needed it.

Derek could tell Dottie was quickly approaching her limit and didn't want to push her. They had talked about safe words, but he hadn't given her one. Maybe now was the time.

"Dottie, I know we talked a little about safe words, and I hope you never have to use one with me, but I want you to know you can. I'm going to give you two words to use. They are words that you wouldn't normally say in this situation. The first one is to slow down, that you need a break or something needs adjusting. When you start to feel that you can't take any more, I want you to say *monkey*."

"*Monkey*? Why monkey?" she asked.

"Because it is not something you would normally say. Sometimes you might say stop or don't and not really mean it. If you say monkey, I will know you are approaching your limit and we need to take a break like we are doing now."

"Okay, monkey it is then. You said two words, why two?"

"As I just explained, the first word, or monkey is to slow down, the second will be to use when you're overwhelmed and can't take any more. It means you're at your limit and need to stop. When you say either word we will stop, but when you say the second word or *elephant*, everything will stop for a while until we figure out why you needed to stop and what happened. Understand?"

Dottie nodded, maybe she should say monkey now. All this was definitely overwhelming her. Was he planning on hurting her so bad that she had to stop him?

Cupping her face in both his hands, Derek leaned down and looked at her. "Dottie, I hope you never have to use either word, but I want you to know that if you ever feel the need or get scared or need something, you have the power to stop everything at any time." Brushing her lips with his, he straightened up and pulled the big dildo out again.

"Now before we start, what are your safe words, and what do they mean?" He was all business now.

"Monkey for slow down and elephant to stop." She answered smartly.

"Very good, now...hmmm....where should I put this?" He wondered, tapping his chin with one finger like he was considering a monumental task.

Dottie didn't answer, thinking the question was more to himself than to her. All she could do was watch him warily.

Derek stood like that for several long seconds before finally seeming to make a decision. "I think we will start with it here and then consider other places it could go. Open your mouth. Since you won't be able to talk if you want me to stop, spread your fingers wide," he told her as he showed her with his hand what he wanted her to do.

After she answered that she understood about the hand signal, he slowly fed the huge dildo into her mouth, then kneeling down in front of her, proceeded to lick and suck her sore and swollen breasts. After he had removed the rope, the blood returning to them made them feel huge, and they throbbed. Soon she was coming again, and again. That was five, surely, he was done. But Derek hadn't given up. He took the huge dildo from her mouth and teased her slit with it after removing both vibes. Slipping it inside her pussy, then just the tip into her rear hole. Dottie came three more times.

After a total of eight orgasms, she was slumped against the cross and not responding to any stimuli.

Derek unfastened her and carried her to a huge tub in the corner of the room. Setting her on a chaise beside the tub, he started it filling and went and got her juice and water.

Holding her up, he helped her drink both bottles, praising her and telling her how good she had been and how proud of her he was, kissing her face gently while he talked.

He left her lying while he quickly stripped, then lifting her, he sat in the tub with her lying between his legs. He soothed the warm water over her, continuing to praise her and placing soft kisses where he could reach. She was perfect.

Dottie lay in his arms, enjoying the warm water and the feel of his hands gently skimming her body. Even though they were both naked, there was nothing sexual in his touch, just a calming feeling and it was very soothing.

Dottie relaxed and let her mind drift, not that she could have concentrated on anything at that point. What Derek had done to her was amazing. She had never thought her body would respond the way it did. Forced orgasms, who knew?

It wasn't something she wanted to do every day, but she had a feeling if she stayed with Derek for very long, she would have more orgasms than she ever imagined. Where was all this going? Where did she want it to go? She had been enjoying being single with the occasional date, but even though it had only been two days, the time she had spent with Derek was perfect. He was kind, considerate, and they had talked and spent some quality time together. It wasn't just all about sex. Most of the guys she had dated had been willing to take her out for a meal or on some activity for the evening, but if she didn't put out, she never heard from them again.

With Derek, he made it all about her. As she was thinking, she realized that Derek had made the afternoon all about her, he hadn't even taken care of himself. She could feel him beneath her as she sat on his lap and even now, he was worried about her and not himself. Time to do something for him.

"Derek, you didn't..." she started hesitantly.

"Honey, I got everything I needed. I don't always need sex. Sometimes, just pleasing my woman is enough for mem" he answered, as he pulled her closer to him.

Turning in his arms, she looked up into his deep, dark brown eyes and said, "Derek, I want to do something for you, will you let me take you in my mouth?"

What man could answer no to that? Derek thought of himself as fairly intelligent and was never one to refuse a lady. "If you want to, sweetheart." He smiled at her.

The fact that she was worried about him and his needs just made her more perfect in his eyes. He could see a future with Ms. Chapman and wondered how she felt about children. That was an issue they needed to address if this went where he thought it would. But now was way too soon, it was only the first weekend, the first of many, he hoped.

Dottie turned around on her knees, and flipping her hair over one shoulder, leaned down to take him in her mouth.

Chapter Seven

Dottie woke later alone in the big bed in Derek's room. He must have carried her up there after they were done in the tub, she remembered taking him in her mouth and swallowing him to completion, and then he held her close to him in the water, warming it several times before she fell asleep.

Looking around, she didn't see Derek anywhere, so she grabbed one of his shirts and went to find him.

He was sitting on the back porch with his laptop, typing furiously. He seemed very focused and she didn't want to disturb him, so she just walked over to the glider and sat down to wait for him to finish.

Derek nodded at Dottie and she smiled, still trying not to disturb him.

He continued typing for several minutes before turning his attention to her.

"Hey, how'd you sleep?" he asked in that deep, gravelly voice of his.

"Good, but Derek, as much as I hate to end this, I need to go home so I can get things ready for work in the morning. As it is, I will probably hear about not calling in all weekend," she told him with a sigh. She really didn't want to end their time together. This weekend had been a fantasy and a dream come true.

Dottie was afraid that when reality hit, she would be in for a letdown. Would she see Derek during the week? They both had busy careers and their hours were not conventional. Could they find time for each other? Would he want to see her? His words and actions indicated he did, but was reality something different? For the first time in a long time, Dottie wasn't sure how to proceed and what to do next.

She really wanted Derek to come home with her and stay but didn't know how to ask.

Derek looked at her with a hint of sadness in his eyes. "I guess you should go to work tomorrow. No chance I can talk you into running away with me?" he asked just a hint of seriousness in his voice.

Dottie stood and walked over to him. Draping herself into his lap, she cupped his face with her hand and looked into his eyes. "That sounds like a wonderful idea, but we both know it won't work. We are both too responsible to do something like that."

"I guess you're right, it was a nice thought. Let's get you dressed and I'll grab my go bag and we'll get something to eat before I take you home," Derek said, lifting her and leading her into the house.

"'Go bag'?" she asked.

"A bag I keep packed in case I have to go in a hurry. Every agent has one. You never know when an assignment will take you out of town and sometimes you have to be ready in a hurry. I keep one here and one at the office. It has enough clothes and other necessities to last me a week. If I need to be away longer than that I can always buy additional supplies."

Dottie was really confused now but didn't say anything, she just went along with him. Maybe he had an assignment out of town for the week and couldn't give her any details.

Derek took Dottie for dinner then drove her home. Her car had been moved from the hotel back to her condo sometime during the weekend, so she had no worries.

Arriving at her condo, Derek grabbed his bag and followed her to the door. Looking at him curiously, she still didn't say anything, just handed him the key to open the door and let him follow her in.

Quickly turning the lights on, she gave him a quick tour. When they reached her bedroom, he set his bag down. Looking at it, she finally asked, "Why do you need that? Are you going away for an assignment?"

Derek simply answered, "no," and walked out to her living room. Sitting on the couch, he kicked off his shoes, put his big feet on her antique coffee table, and grabbed the remote, flipping through the channels until he found a football game.

Dottie looked at him incredulously and sat beside him. "Do you mind telling me what's going on here?" she asked.

Grinning and not turning his attention away from the game, he told her, "You're my next assignment. I'm staying here. The couch doesn't look big enough for me, so I'll have to sleep in your bed. Whether you sleep there or somewhere else is up to you."

Grabbing the remote out of his hand, she clicked off the television and demanded, "Would you stop watching that and tell me what's going on?"

Still grinning like a fool, Derek explained, very proud of himself. "The powers that be have decided that you are in danger. I have been assigned to protect you. I could have used the entire team, but as a hardship to myself I decided to take the assignment solo and will stay with you until it is determined that the threat is over."

"Wait a minute, I've been threatened. Round-the-clock protection, by who? How? What the hell is going on?" She was starting to get mad and a little scared.

"The General didn't say much, but what he did say threatened your safety. Also, members of his staff confirmed that you were a target. Did you know that he requested the interview and specifically asked for you by name? Somehow you got on his radar and he has decided that he wants you. I am here to prevent that. If you don't want me, I can assign other members of the team, but I would really, really like to be the one to protect you. Would it be a hardship to have me in your life for a few weeks?"

Weeks, she thought, danger, the General had specifically targeted her. Her head was reeling, and she couldn't think. Was she really in danger or was this something Derek was making up to be close to her? She didn't think he would make something like this up and she could vaguely remember the General saying something as Derek carried her out of the room, but it was all a blur.

Leaning back on the couch, she closed her eyes to think and try to decide what to do. If Derek was going to be her bodyguard around the clock, she was going to have to make some major changes to her life. She wasn't sure if she wanted to do that.

As if he had read her mind, Derek turned her toward him and said, "I know this is upsetting, but I don't want you to change your routine or your life. If it is too difficult for you having me this close this soon, I can assign other members of the team and we will watch you remotely. You won't even know we are there. I don't want to upset you or this to be any more of an upset to your life than it has to be. I will go to your office but will observe from outside at all times. I would like to be in your home with you, but if that is too uncomfortable, I can watch from the street, I don't have to be in your bed, although that's where I'd like to be. Dottie, you tell me what you want."

Still reeling, Dottie stood and said, "I'm going to take a hot bath and think. Don't come in there." And she walked away.

Turning the game back on, Derek relaxed back onto the couch. *Well, at least she hasn't thrown me out yet,* he thought. He probably could have handled telling her differently. He hoped by keeping things light, he wouldn't scare her too badly. The threat from the general was real and whether she liked it on not she was getting round-the-clock protection. Whether it was him or his team remained to be seen.

Deciding he was thirsty, he went to the kitchen to look for a beer. Finding nothing but mineral water and juice, he called one of the guys and had him run for a case. If he was staying here, he needed provisions.

What he hadn't told Dottie was that along with himself, the team was also going to be observing her. The threat was bigger than he had told her. Whether she was aware of it or not, she was in possession of information the General wanted and wanted badly. Their sources had indicated that he would stop at nothing to get this information. Part of Derek's assignment was to see if he could figure out what she knew and determine what kind of threat it posed. There was more to Ms. Dorothy Chapman than what showed on the surface, and he was going to discover it if it took the rest of his life.

Chapter Eight

Dottie sat for a long time in the tub, thinking. This was what she wanted. She had wanted Derek to come home with her. Why was she so upset? She knew Derek would take care of her and she didn't need to worry about the General or his men. Derek would keep her safe. He told her that he would interfere in her life as little as possible. Would she really be able to go about her normal routine knowing he was watching her every move? How could he not intrude? All she could do was try and see what happened. She really did like the idea of him being with her.

Her mind made up, Dottie finished in the bathroom and found one of her sexier nightgowns to put on. Might as well take advantage of the situation while she could.

Walking seductively, she hoped, she sauntered out to the living room to find Derek where she had left him, only with a can of beer in his hand.

"Where did you get that? I know I don't have any," she asked as she walked up to him. Looks like he's already making himself at home.

"Delivery," he answered, patting the spot next to him.

She sat and he pulled her closer, wrapping one arm around her. "I didn't know they delivered here."

"I know a guy," he answered, apparently engrossed in the game.

Taking the beer, she took a deep drag, and shaking her head, said, "I'm going to bed. I go to the gym at five and need to sleep. Are you coming?" she said, hoping he would and she would, too.

"I'm gonna watch the end of this, then I'll be in." He took his attention away from the game long enough to kiss her thoroughly, then smacked her on the ass as she walked away.

A little disappointed, Dottie took herself to bed and crawled to the far side, leaving room for Derek. Her bed wasn't as big as his, but she did have a king size and it was roomy.

She must have fallen asleep. Next thing she knew, Derek was crawling in bed and pulled her to him. She thought he might try to make love to her, but he just slipped one hand over a breast and laid the other between her legs, and snuggled up to her. Soon he was snoring and she lay awake.

Dottie lay there for what seemed like hours before she fell asleep. Soon the alarm went off and it was time to start her day. Derek had told her not to change her routine and her routine was to work out in the building gym every day at five a.m. She got herself untangled from Derek and headed for her workout clothes. She really didn't feel like working out but knew that missing one day led to two and before you knew it, the routine was gone.

Derek rolled over and watched her dress. It looked like she was putting on gym clothes so he asked, "Working out, baby?" as he sat up and grabbed his go bag which he had placed beside the bed.

He had thought about waking her last night but held himself back. Just sleeping next to her was torture, but he didn't know how she would have responded and didn't want to push the issue.

"Yeah, I do every morning," she answered, yawning.

"Great, I'll go with you."

Dottie didn't answer him, just headed for the kitchen to make coffee. She really needed it this morning.

Derek had told her he didn't want to interrupt her routine, so she kept to it as much as possible. It was a little distracting having him follow her everywhere, but true to his word, he didn't interfere.

After the workout, she got ready for work and Derek followed her, letting her make the drive herself.

Her day went normally and Derek observed from outside. After the awkwardness of the first day, the week fell into a routine and other than Derek being with her in the evening, nothing was out of place. Her week was quiet with no activities scheduled and she enjoyed spending her evenings and nights with him. By Friday, it felt normal for him to be with her.

Even though he'd been with her every day, she'd been able to carve out some time to do some internet research on BDSM and felt more comfortable with what he wanted now. She still had questions and had found some groups to post those questions in until she felt she could ask Derek.

She'd discovered that everything he'd told her was right and from what she'd learned in the chat groups, he was a good Dom and was doing everything right.

On Friday, Derek changed it up a little by offering to drive her to work instead of following her. They had decided to spend the weekend at his house and he wanted to go straight there from her work. Dottie agreed.

On the drive out of the city, Derek asked her, "Dottie, would you come to the club with me tonight? I just want to show you around and introduce you to some of my friends. We won't do anything you don't want to. I haven't been there for over two weeks and I really need to check-in. I keep in touch with the manager via phone and e-mail, but I like to put in an appearance occasionally. Would you go with me?"

Dottie couldn't find a reason not to go and she was curious. "What will I wear?" she asked, not sure what people wore to this type of club.

"We'll find you something." He grinned.

When they reached Derek's place, they greeted the horses first before going into the house. Derek fixed them a quick dinner while Dottie finished a few things on her laptop.

After eating, Derek led her to the bedroom, and pulling a package out of the closet, handed it to her.

Wait. He'd been with her all week. How had he gone shopping and had a package delivered inside his house?

He saw the question on her face. "While you were in your weekly briefing, Tyler took my place so I could go shopping and run out here. I checked on the horses and was back before your meeting was over.

Dottie nodded. Every Wednesday they had a briefing that took several hours. It made sense that she hadn't noticed his absence.

Opening the package, Dottie found a dark purple brassiere and matching boy shorts. That was all that was in the package. "You want me to wear this?" she asked, continuing to look in the package, sure there was more in there.

Derek took the small bag out of her hands and grasped both her hands in his. "Please," was all he said.

Nodding, Dottie sat to change. Putting the outfit on didn't take long, and when she was done, she walked into the bathroom to check her appearance. She actually looked good. This was something she would never have considered wearing outside the house, but it was a very flattering color and her legs looked long and sleek.

Leaving her hair down, she arranged it over her shoulders, helping to cover her chest. When she came out of the bathroom, Derek was waiting, wearing black jeans and a black leather vest with military books. Very much the alpha male.

Letting out a wolf whistle, he twirled her around, smacking her on the ass. "Looking hot, baby," he told her. "I'm going to have to keep you close all night or someone will take you away from me and I can't have that," he said possessively.

Pulling a thin band with a heart that matched her outfit and had his initials on it out of his pocket, he fastened it around her neck. "This will act as a temporary collar tonight. One day I hope you will wear my collar permanently, but for tonight this will have to do. It will tell people that you belong to me. No one should talk to you without my permission, and you will talk to no one without my permission. The rules in the club are very simple. As my sub, even if only for one night, you belong to me. You do nothing without my approval while in the club. I know this will be hard for you, but it's for your safety. If you do something that offends another Dom or his sub, he will want you punished and by the club rules, he has the right to. No one touches you but me, and I won't allow you to be punished by another Dom. If you follow the rules, this will not be an issue. I will stay with you and guide you tonight. Before we go in the club, there's a contract for you to read and sign. I have one here so we can do this before we leave. Honey, you will do fine, don't be nervous," as he said the last word, he pulled her into his arms and held her tight.

He led her into the kitchen and sat her at the bar to read and sign the contract while he went to the dungeon to pack his toy bag. He planned on taking Dottie to a private room for some play after he finished showing her around.

Chapter Nine

The week had been quiet and there was little activity from the General, but Derek wasn't ready to let his guard down. He still didn't trust things, it was too quiet.

But now was not the time to worry about the General. He was taking Dottie to his club and he needed to set down some rules. She had read the contract and knew all the club rules, but he had a few personal rules he wanted her to follow as his sub, even if it was only for one night. He would tell her in the truck.

For the trip to the club, he pulled out big blue, his personal monster truck. Opening the door, he helped her up and in and had her scoot to the middle before crawling in himself. Making sure she was secured before fastening his own belt, he started them on the way.

"Dottie, in addition to the rules for the club which were in the contract you signed, I have a few personal rules as a Dom that I want my subs to follow. The first one is no speaking without permission, even to me. If you want to say something, you may touch my arm and I will give you permission to speak, other than that you are to be quiet at all times. The second rule is you do not touch, shake hands, or anything with anyone but me. If I want you to shake hands I will let you know. Third, no looking at any other Dom or Domme in the eye. You will be able to tell the Doms and Dommes by their apparel. Subs, male, and female, will be dressed similarly to you, and Doms and Dommes will be dressed similarly to me. Do you have any questions?"

Yeah, I have questions, Mister. Number one, who do you think you are, and what the hell do you mean I have to follow rules? Dottie thought to herself, but being a smart woman, said, "I'm not sure why I have to do these things. What does it matter who I talk to or if I shake hands and if I look people in the eyes?"

Dottie saw him take a deep breath before he answered. Had she made him mad?

"Dottie, in a Dom/sub relationship, I make the rules, you follow them. I don't want you offending anyone accidentally by saying or doing the wrong thing. I know you're a smart, intelligent woman, but this is a totally new environment for you and you have no idea what you're getting into or how to behave in this world. If you have set rules, it will make you more comfortable. Now instead of not knowing how to respond to something someone may say that may make you uncomfortable, you have the excuse that your Dom won't allow you to talk and don't have to answer. Most of the people you meet tonight will know that I am one of the owners and will expect you to behave in a certain way because they know that is the way I expect my subs to behave. No one will think anything less of you and they will respect you more for following my rules. The rules are to protect you, not to humiliate or make you feel less of yourself. Can you do this for me?"

Dottie thought a moment. What Derek had said made sense and he wasn't really asking that much of her. If the rules were truly for her protection, then it made sense to do what he said.

"Will everyone else be doing the same?" she asked, curious if she was the only one who had to follow rules.

"Each Dom has his own rules for his sub, and they are all different. Everyone in the club has to follow the rules on the contract you signed or they get their membership put on probation or revoked depending on what they do, but the rules for individual subs depend on the Doms. Some subs will kneel and crawl and not walk in their Master's presence, some will wear a gag. There are all kinds of rules for different situations. If you just do as I have asked you, you will be fine."

He wanted to reassure her but keep her scared enough to obey him. Derek wasn't really worried about Dottie, he knew she could do what he asked and that there wouldn't be a problem.

Derek had taken subs to the club before, but never anyone he was as serious about as Dottie. He wanted to show her off and proclaim to the world that she was his and his alone, and if anyone even thought about looking at her too long or touching her there would be hell to pay.

Derek had given Dottie a leather jacket of his to wear, which was too big, but looked good on her and covered her from her shoulders to mid-thigh. She looked hot.

Taking her in the club, he gave her paperwork to the receptionist, then showed her where the locker rooms were. He took her to his office to leave her jacket. He sat her on the couch in his office and gave her a brief description of what the club would look like and what she was likely to see so she wouldn't be shocked. Leaving his toy bag on the couch, he led her out to look around.

The night was early and it was quiet, not a lot of activities or guests happening yet. It would be busier later, but Derek had planned on getting there before the crowd so he could show Dottie around. Friday and Saturday night were normally the busiest, but most of the activity happened later.

Derek showed her the various play stations and stages where there were demonstrations. Then he took her to the bar and introduced her to the bartender, explaining that there was a two-drink limit.

The bartender looked familiar, but Dottie couldn't place him. "Hey, Dottie, you remember me? Tyler, we met last Friday."

"God, you idiot, don't remind her of that. Dottie, he was one of the agents at Quantico, and he's one of my partners here. You can say hi and talk to him."

"Yeah, Dottie, don't talk without permission, he'll wallop on your ass if you do," Tyler told her.

Dottie didn't know if he was teasing or not, so she just smiled and said, "Hi."

After introducing her to several people at the bar, including Tracy and Dillon, who had conducted her forensic interview, he took her back to his office.

Grabbing his toy bag, he led her to the private rooms. "There are several themed rooms for role play," he told her as he showed her a room that looked like a sultan's tent in the desert, a Victorian room, a medical room, a schoolroom, and several others.

"Any fantasy you want to play we can, and if we don't have a room outfitted for it, we have a huge prop room and can accommodate almost anything in one of the plain rooms."

Dottie just nodded and smiled, wondering where he was taking her and what he had planned for the night.

After he finished showing her all the rooms, Derek led her back to the medical room. "I reserved this for tonight," he told her, grinning. "I think you need a touch up on the shave I gave you last weekend, and a rectal exam by the doctor is in need."

Leading her into the room, he told her, "I want you to strip and put this on." Handing her a hospital gown, he said, "Open in the front, don't tie it, then get up on the table and put your legs in the stirrups. I'll adjust them so that they are comfortable for you."

As he was saying this, he was removing his clothing and putting on doctor's scrubs, apparently, he was taking this fantasy thing seriously.

Dottie followed his instructions and was soon on the table, legs spread in the stirrups just as instructed.

Derek walked up to her and said, "I see you are due for your annual exam, Ms. Chapman, any complaints I need to know about?"

Smiling and getting into her role, Dottie answered, "Oh, Dr. Moore, I been having the biggest pain in my ass." She almost giggled.

"Well, Ms. Chapman, I'll make sure we look at that, but before I do. I believe we should shave you to make sure I can see everything I need to."

Remembering the experience in the shower, Dottie grinned and answered, "Thank you, Dr. Moore."

Derek walked away from her and she could hear water running and objects being placed on some surface. Soon he was back with a metal cart, on which she could see a bowl of water and could tell there were several objects under a towel.

Whistling, Derek moved so that he was standing between her legs and placed a warm towel over her mound. Walking to her side, he parted her gown and asked, "Have you had a breast exam in the last year, Ms. Chapman?"

"No, Dr. Moore," Dottie answered. This was more fun than she thought it would be. Imagine a grown-up game of doctor. She never played it this way when she was a kid.

Derek pulled on a pair of latex exam gloves and said, "Relax, Ms. Chapman, this won't hurt, much."

Dottie shivered in anticipation as he gently placed a hand on each breast. He moved his hands slowly around her breasts until he had touched every inch, working from the base to the nipples. When he reached her nipples he pinched and pulled them, bringing them to taut peaks. "I believe these need a little extra attention, Ms. Chapman." He grinned and leaned down to take a nipple in his mouth while pinching and pulling the other one.

When he had Dottie moaning and writhing on the table, he pulled a pair of nipple clamps out of his pocket, applying them quickly, he walked to stand between her legs again.

Him and his pockets, she thought, remembering her afternoon on the cross and how he kept finding objects to torture her with in those pockets.

Derek was standing between her legs and she couldn't see what he was doing. He had moved the table behind him and she had no idea what he was up to.

Standing between Dottie's legs, Derek couldn't believe how beautiful she was and that, for now at least, she was his. He was going to work on making that permanent. He would have her, forever.

Pulling the towel off the things he had placed on the table, Derek picked a medium-sized butt plug and a tube of lube. Looking at Dottie, he said, "I believe you said you needed a rectal exam, Ms. Chapman?"

"Yes, Doctor," Dottie squealed as he pushed a lubed finger into her bottom hole. He'd been having her use a different plug every evening for an hour or so and she was growing more comfortable with anal play.

Arching off the table, Dottie moaned and closed her eyes. What was this man going to do to her?

"Ms. Chapman, I believe this hole needs a little stretching before I can perform a thorough exam. I'm going to insert a plug before we do your shave and pelvic."

Derek put words to action and slowly inserted the plug, Dottie writhing and moaning the entire time. When he had the plug inserted, he shaved her, spreading the mentholated cream over her mound and clit, teasing, and playing with her bringing her closer and closer to the release her body so desperately craved.

When he had her shaved and had wiped her clean with a hot, damp cloth, he leaned down and ran his tongue over her newly shaven skin.

The feeling was incredible. Until he had shaved her last week, Dottie hadn't known what the experience was like. It made her more aware of the area and everything down there was more sensitive. When she was wearing clothes, every brush of the fabric was teasing, and she was in a state of arousal constantly. Derek made her very aware of her body and what it was capable of.

"I believe you're due for a pelvic exam, Ms. Chapman. Is that correct?" he asked in a cool professional voice.

"Yes, Dr. Moore," she answered him, trying not to giggle. This was more fun than she had ever thought it would be. None of her other lovers would have ever done anything like this. Thinking of the other rooms Derek had shown her, she wondered what other games they could and would play. Maybe something historical with costumes, or she had always thought being a slave girl would be fun. She would have to ask Derek.

Right now, she needed to pay attention, as Derek was again doing something between her legs.

Raising an object in his hand, Derek showed her a large glass dildo. "I have this new device for pelvic exams. I'm going to be using this on your pussy and clit. Hold very still, Ms. Chapman, it may be cold."

Derek knew it was cold. He had had it sitting in ice water since he started the breast exam, but Dottie couldn't see that from her position.

Taking the dildo, he tapped her clit with it.

"Fuck that's cold!" Dottie screamed.

"I'm so sorry, Ms. Chapman, it should warm soon," he said with an evil grin as he stroked the icy thing over her folds, circling her pussy with it.

"Oh, God, Dr. Moore, that's so cold." Dottie almost screamed as he slowly pushed it inside her.

"Yes, baby, it is, isn't it?" He started pushing the icy dildo into her while pulling the plug out with his other hand.

As he pulled the plug out, Dottie thought, *Oh my God, he's not going to put that icy thing there, there is no way.* Which is exactly what he did. Dottie arched and screamed as he pushed the icy dildo into her rear hole. It was larger than the plug and she jerked trying to get away from the huge, cold thing.

Derek laid one hand on her stomach to hold her still and said, "Relax, you can take it, relax," looking into her eyes intently.

Dottie took several deep breaths and tried to relax, but every fiber of her being was fighting the cold, icy thing going into her ass.

"God, Derek, I can't take it. Oh, God." She moaned, wanting him to stop, but part of her also wanted him to continue.

"*Sshh,* you can do this, *shh.*" He soothed her, slowly and relentlessly pushing the dildo in her ass.

Finally, he had it in as far as he wanted and he started rubbing, pulling, and twisting her clit with one hand and flicking the clamps on her nipples with the other. "Come for me, Dottie, show me how much you like having your ass stuffed." Plunging two fingers into her pussy while pressing on her clit with his thumb, he could tell by the change in her moans and the way her body was moving that she was close. He pulled his two fingers out and shoved three inside her, fucking them rapidly in and out until she screamed her release.

Leaning down, he kissed her gently and soothed a hand over her face. Dottie panted and tried to catch her breath. How could each time he made her come be more incredible than the last?

Derek slowly pulled the dildo out of her bottom and put it on the tray behind him to clean later. Trailing his hand through her folds, he pinched her clit again.

"You're so hot, baby, even filled with ice, this little ass is hot. Now I'm going to fill your pussy and then I'm taking that ass. Are you ready, baby?" As he spoke, he continued pinching and pulling her clit.

Dottie groaned and arched her back, not able to respond, not sure she was ready for this.

Derek took another dildo off the table and slowly pushed it into her pussy, filling her there. Then he grabbed a condom and rolled it on before taking the lube and lubing her rear hole. Fitting himself to her, he began slowly pushing himself in.

"Oh, Derek, it's so big, it burns, oh, oh, oh." She tried to pull away. He was bigger than anything she had had in there and the stretching of those tissues burned.

Derek slowly continued pushing himself inside her, she was so tight. Once he was in to the hilt, he reached up and started flicking her nipple clamps again, leaning over her to take her mouth in a possessive kiss.

Slowly pulling out, he pushed back giving her time to adjust to having both her holes filled. Continuing the kiss, he swept his tongue through her mouth.

As he felt her relax, he started moving in and out of her faster and with more force until he established a punishing rhythm. Feeling her body tense and knowing she was close, he reached with both hands and pulled off the clamps as her orgasm started.

She screamed into his mouth and he pounded her until he reached his completion and she came again.

Laying over her with his head on her chest, he gathered her in his arms and held her until they had both recovered a little.

Relaxing, he picked her up and carried her to the small settee in the corner, wrapping her in a soft blanket. Then he gave her the water and juice that he had placed there earlier and held her close. Murmuring soothing words to her and stroking her hair and back, telling her how wonderful she was and how much she meant to him.

Dottie relaxed into Derek, enjoying his closeness. She loved the time he spent with her after their play, whether he sat and cuddled here or in the tub in his playroom.

Working one hand free of the blanket he had wrapped her in, she placed her palm on his chest and looked deep into his eyes and quietly said, "Mr. Derek Moore, I think I'm falling in love with you."

Derek didn't react for a minute and she wasn't sure he had heard her at first, until he finally said, "Ms. Dorothy Chapman, I believe I am in love with you."

Derek had never told another woman he loved her before and never would again. In the short week, they had been together, Dottie had become his life. He couldn't imagine being without her. When he heard her say she felt the same way, his heart swelled and it felt too big for his chest. She burrowed closer to him and he held her tight.

They sat like that for a long time, him holding and rocking her in his arms, Dottie placing soft kisses on his chest. After sitting for a while,

Derek lifted Dottie and stood her up. He walked her to the shower in the room and stripping off his scrubs and pulling her gown off her shoulders, walked into the shower with her. Washing her thoroughly, he continued praising her and telling her how beautiful she was. They finished and he dried her and helped her dress. Quickly dressing himself, he led her back to his office to get her jacket.

Dottie was still in a daze as she let him wash and dress her. He wrapped on arm around her and led her out of the club and back to his truck, driving them back to his home.

"Dottie, I want you to think about moving in with me. We can keep your condo for a place to stay during the week when we both have to be in the city, but I want you with me all the time."

Dottie was still in a daze but smiled and nodded. Yes, she wanted this.

They arrived at Derek's house and he led her in. Grabbing a couple glasses and some wine, he headed for the living room to sit and relax with his woman. He wanted her close.

As he walked by the counter, he noticed his phone, beeping with a message. Cursing, he grabbed it, knowing it had to be something important or the team would have handled it.

Checking the message, it was Dillon. Dillon and Tracy had been the second shift watching Dottie's condo that night and he was afraid the news was not good.

He was correct. In the message, Dillon said that Dottie's condo had been broken into and the place was a total wreck. Whoever had done it had made a total mess of the place and it was impossible for the team to tell if anything was missing. Dillon had said that the place was such a disaster that he wasn't sure Dottie would be able to tell.

Derek was totally pissed. The purpose of having the team on twenty-four-hour duty was to prevent something like this from happening. He was going to have someone's ass. Now he had to ruin her evening and go tell Dottie.

Sitting on the couch and pulling her toward him, he handed her a glass of wine before taking a big drink himself. What he could use was a shot, but that would come later.

Dottie sipped her wine and looked a Derek, something was bothering him. "Derek, what's wrong?"

"Dottie, I have bad news, someone broke into your condo tonight and trashed it. Dillon and Tracy are there, but the place is so bad they can't tell if anything is missing. We need to go and see if you can tell what might be missing. Do you know of anything you might have that someone would want?"

"Derek, you've been there, you know I don't have anything really valuable, other than my laptop and it only has my files for work on it. I keep all my personal data on the PC in my room. The computers are the most valuable."

Derek made a quick call to Dillon and both computers were gone. Luckily, Dottie had backed up both her laptop and home PC on flash drives and kept two copies, one in her purse and one at the office. She willingly gave Derek the flash drives she had with her and he planned on going through them as soon as he had her settled and sleeping.

They quickly changed clothes and Derek drove her to her condo to survey the damage and make sure nothing else was missing.

The place looked like a tornado had hit it. Derek walked Dottie through the mess and when he felt she was calm enough, left her looking around while he tore Dillon and Tracy a new one.

"What the fuck happened?" He growled the minute he had them outside.

"Boss, I don't know. I swear we did not leave this spot all night, and one of us had eyes on the front at all times."

"What about the back and the windows?" Derek demanded.

Dillon and Tracy exchanged a glance and both hung their heads. "We watched what we could see from our vantage point, but that was all."

"You didn't think of splitting up so one of you could watch the front and the other could watch the back?" Derek practically screamed.

"Uh...no," Dillon answered. He didn't want to tell Derek that he and Tracy had been arguing and not really watching that closely. Dillon had been after Tracy for several months and really wanted her. Tracy was fighting him at every opportunity and he had hoped taking this assignment would give them some time together and he would be able to convince her to go out with him. So far all they had done was fight.

Dillon really wanted a chance with Tracy, and when Dottie's apartment was being ransacked, they had been arguing about her going out with him. He couldn't understand why she was so reluctant. She was smart and sassy, exactly his type.

They had played several times at the club together and he didn't understand why she wouldn't take it further. He was determined to have his way. The next time they played at the club, she was in for a surprise. Right now he had Derek to deal with though. He had really fucked up this time.

Derek couldn't believe what he was hearing and just shook his head. "I expect a full report by 8 a.m. and no excuses. You're both dismissed, for now, we'll deal with this tomorrow," he told them as he stormed off. He couldn't believe the incompetence he was surrounded by sometimes.

Chapter Ten

Derek stomped off, wanting to get back to Dottie. He had left her looking somewhat dazed and overwhelmed. She had said she was okay, but Derek had his doubts. If he hadn't needed to find out what was going on he wouldn't have left her.

Derek walked back into the condo and found Dottie sitting on the floor looking at a picture that had been destroyed. She had tears in her eyes.

Sitting beside her, he pulled her into his lap and held her. The picture she held looked like it could have been her mother and it had been wadded up and torn, a deliberate move.

"This was the last picture I had of her. Then she was gone," Dottie said quietly.

"Honey, we'll get it restored and it will look just the way you remember it." Derek didn't know for sure how he was going to accomplish that, but he would.

"I can't find all the pieces, all I have is this." And then the dam broke and she started sobbing in earnest. "We weren't close in the last few years. I still miss them though. Mom especially."

Derek just held her close and let her cry. He would get a team to clean her condo and repair everything that could be, replace what they could, and trash the rest. He would fix this for her.

Standing up with her in his arms, he said, "Come on honey, let's get you out of here. We'll get this cleaned up and then you and I will go through and see what's missing. I don't know what I was thinking, bringing you here tonight."

Dottie reached up and touched his face, trying to smile through her tears. "Thank you for bringing me and being here. I needed to see."

Derek had given Dillon the flash drives to copy before he dismissed him, and Dillon was standing at the door with the copies for him.

Dillon and Tracy would be up all night writing reports and analyzing the drives for information.

Derek took the drives and slipped them in his pocket, not letting go of Dottie. Dillon could see the hurt in his eyes and his guilt compounded. He should have never been fighting with Tracy and if he had followed procedure and had split up with her instead of insisting she stay with him, this would have never happened. Why did he have to listen to his cock anyway? Walking to the car where Tracy was waiting, he knew they were both in for a long night, and with her mad at him on top of it, things were all fucked up.

During the forty-five-minute drive back to Derek's home, Dottie was quiet, so quiet Derek was worried about her. He was starting to think maybe she had gone into shock when she finally sighed and said, "What did I do to deserve this? I didn't have much, but I worked hard for what I have and to get where I am. Why would someone want to do something like this to me?"

Derek's heart was breaking for her. Not sure he was saying the right thing, he said all he could think of. "Baby, it's not your fault. I will find out who is responsible for this and we will make them pay. I have a team cleaning up your condo and we will salvage everything we can." He wished he could fix it but knew he couldn't.

She just sat quietly the rest of the way to his house. When they arrived, instead of walking to the door, she went to the horses, Derek following her.

"Do you want to go for a ride? Would that help you settle?"

"Yes, can we? I always used to ride when I was upset at home." She had a hint of excitement in her voice and as she was talking, Patrice walked up to her to nuzzle her neck.

"Oh, look, Derek, she knows I'm upset, can we take them out?"

"Yes, let's go. I want to get jackets, it's cool. Can you get Patrice saddled while I'm gone?"

Nodding enthusiastically, she went into the barn, the horse following beside her.

Derek was glad she was responding better, he would take her to the park and they would take a long ride. There was a path there that the horses were used to and they could go pretty fast. The horses needed the run anyway.

Derek went into the house to get jackets and make a quick phone call. He wanted to make sure the team was continuing to watch the condo and have someone check on Dottie's office. He had a bad feeling.

Placing the flash drives in a locked drawer, he made sure his house was secure and turned the alarm on. Something was not right. He had felt like they had been followed, and wasn't taking any chances.

Grabbing a couple jackets, he hurried back to the barn. It was quiet outside, almost too quiet. He should have heard the horses and Dottie talking to Patrice, some type of noise.

Going on instinct, Derek crept silently into the barn. Still nothing. The horses should have neighed in recognition when he entered the barn, they always did. Something was up. He kept quiet and slid silently against the wall, listening intently.

The barn was small, with eight stalls and a tack room. He had never had more than two horses and was planning for more when he retired. The extra stalls were used for storage or empty at this point. He came to Big Al's stall, and the horse lay on his side. Sliding in, he saw he was breathing, but not moving. More concerned about Dottie, he left the big animal and kept moving toward the end of the barn. The stall where Patrice should have been was empty, but he heard voices, one of them was male and the other was Dottie's.

"I don't know, I told you I don't know. Please don't hurt her. Please." Dottie was sobbing.

Derek had pushed the panic button on his phone that would alert the team and police before he entered the barn, but it could take a while for backup to get this far out. Even though he was a big man, he could move quickly and silently, so he continued toward the voices, gun drawn.

Crouching down, he crept silently toward the sound, trying to be invisible. He came to the last stall in the barn and the source of the sounds.

Dottie was tied to a chair and a man was standing, holding Patrice's bridle, a knife to her throat. "Tell me the information I want, Ms. Chapman, and I will let you and the horse live, otherwise I'm afraid I may have to do something unpleasant," the man said in a calm, cultured voice as he brandished the knife and looked at Dottie in a hostile manner.

Dottie visibly shuddered and again pleaded. "I told you I don't know. What do you want of me?"

Assessing the situation, Derek weighed his options. He could follow procedure and wait for back-up, risking not only Patrice, but Dottie also. Not an option. All he could think was that he had to get to her and damned the consequences. Listening for a few long moments to make sure there was only one assailant, he formulated his plan.

Moving with stealth and speed despite his size, he waited until Dottie's attacker had his back to him and made his attack. Dottie screamed his name as she saw him approach and smartly flipped her chair to the side when the man lunged for her with the knife.

In the chaos that happened next, Dottie wasn't sure how, but Derek had the man on the ground, he was now in possession of the knife and was sitting on the man's chest. A quick punch to the man's face and he was out cold. Derek quickly tied him up and then went to free Dottie.

By now they could hear sirens approaching and shouts coming from outside. Leaving the man tied on the floor, Derek wrapped an arm around Dottie and walked her out of the barn and into the fray of FBI, police, and rescue personnel.

Chapter Eleven

Dottie woke the next day crushed to Derek's side in his bed. She couldn't believe all that had happened. Parts of it were like a nightmare, and other parts a dream. In the matter of a few hours, she and Derek had played in the club, he had told her he was in love with her, her condo had been broken into, and she had been attacked. She was amazed she had been able to sleep, but after everyone had cleared out, she had fallen into bed with Derek and slept the sleep of the dead. She didn't even remember dreaming. What time was it?

Derek had made her call off work for the rest of the week, not wanting her out of his sight for a few days. Looking at the clock it was early, very early and they had not gotten to bed until very late. She had only slept a couple hours. Derek was still out. Snuggling closer to him, she went back to sleep.

* * * *

Monday morning Derek had gone to the office to file his report and review the statements from his team and the residents of her apartment building. There had to be something he was missing. Dottie insisted she had no idea what information she was being targeted for. There had to be something he was missing. He had a forensic technician going over the thumb drives she kept her files on looking for anything that stood out. With nothing more he could do at this point, he took the next week off to stay with Dottie at the ranch. He didn't trust anyone else to do it at this point.

They spent the time riding and getting to know each other. They had played in the playroom and Derek was introducing her to his world, and she was learning more about being his submissive in and out of the playroom.

Thursday night, they had had an intense session in the playroom and Dottie had fallen into an exhausted sleep before Derek had her out of the tub. She didn't remember him carrying her to bed, but when she woke, he was wrapped around her and they were in his bed.

She lay there going over everything in her mind that had happened in the past few days when she heard her cell phone ringing. Struggling to free herself, she padded naked to the kitchen where she had left her purse. Finding the phone which had stopped ringing by now, she saw it was her office that had called.

Deciding to make coffee before she made her phone call, she went back to Derek's room to get one of his shirts. He was still sleeping.

Dottie went back to the kitchen and started the coffee before checking her messages. There were several, all from her boss. The first few were fairly tame, just acknowledging her need for the rest of the week off and a request to call. As the messages went on, the requests became demands and her boss, Matt, sounded more and more frantic.

By the time she got to the final message, he was screaming and yelling. Dottie quickly dialed his direct line.

Matt answered even more frantic. "Thank God! Dottie, I heard everything that had happened and we were all worried. I also have more bad news."

"Oh God, Matt, I don't think I can take anymore," Dottie said sitting down. What the hell was going on?

Matt quickly informed her that the office had been ransacked and the chaos was centered mostly around her and her partner Terrance Mason's desk. Like her apartment, the damage was so destructive that they couldn't tell if anything was missing or not. Dottie promised to be in as soon as she could and sat at the table, her face in her hands, which is how Derek found her several minutes later.

"What's up?" he asked laying a hand on her back.

Dottie quickly told him about the phone call she had received and that she needed to get to the office. "Will you go with me? I don't want to do this alone and have to face all those stares by myself."

Derek agreed and they dressed to go, planning on eating on the way.

Chapter Twelve

When they got to Dottie's office, the place was still in a state of chaos. Along with all the usual workers, there was police, FBI, and Derek's Secret Service team there. Most of the FBI were people from the group Derek was working with, but the cops were also there.

Between Dottie and Derek, they knew almost everyone there except for one person, James Preston. He was new to the police force, having transferred into his position. He was a pompous asshole.

"Where were you last night, Ms. Chapman?" he asked arrogantly, pulling her arm to pull her away from Derek. He was short and fat, shorter than Dottie by a few inches and over a foot shorter than Derek.

Dottie resisted his pulling and Derek wrapped an arm around her. "She was with me at my house for the last several days, Officer Preston," Derek answered just as arrogantly. It was on!

"And you would be... Sir?" Preston asked, looking up at Derek.

"Special Officer Derek Moore, Secret Service protection division. Ms. Chapman is under the protection of myself and my team, and I or a member of my team have been with her every hour of every day. Does that answer your question?" The man didn't need to know the details of Dottie's protection services.

"Why would a simple reporter need Secret Service protection round the clock? Seems like a waste of the taxpayers' money to me." The little weasel looked at Derek like he was an idiot.

Derek blew out the breath he had been holding and answered, "That is classified," holding Dottie tighter to him.

"Not so classified that I can't find out," Preston said, walking away with his radio.

Derek knew the arrogant jerk wasn't going to find anything out. Turning his back to the twerp, he walked Dottie to her desk area to check for missing items.

Still holding the radio mic in his hand, Officer Preston hurried back to Dottie and Derek. "Hey, I didn't dismiss you." He practically squealed.

Derek just ignored the squawking man. Looking at Dottie, he sat her down at what was left of her desk and said, "Honey, why don't you try and figure out what might be missing while Officer Preston, his superiors, and I all have a talk." Derek was dealing with this ass and now. When he was done, the jerk was going to be back on street patrol.

* * * *

When Derek walked back to where Dottie was sitting, he was alone. A couple quick phone calls on his part and a quick talk with a few supervisors and bye-bye officer Preston. With that stress gone, he could concentrate on Dottie.

She was sitting at her desk, her head in her hands again. Walking up behind her, he started rubbing her shoulders and back soothingly. "Have you found anything missing,?" he asked, quietly trying to keep some calm.

"Both my flash drives are gone, all my personal pictures and everything I've been working on for the past months. All the information on the General, all my stories, everything," she answered, shaking her head, and wringing her hands.

"Was all that stuff backed up on the drives you had in your purse?" he asked, still trying to keep his voice calm.

"Everything but the work I did the Friday I interviewed the General. My notes from that night are still at your place, I haven't taken time to transcribe them." Her voice was full of despair. Losing her work wasn't really a big deal, she did have backups, but her pictures and some of her personal things really bothered her. Most of the pictures were her only copies. They were just pictures of her with various celebrities and dignitaries, but it was her history. The story of her career. Her climb up the ladder.

She was proud of how far she had come. The pictures showed her in various countries on assignment and held a lot of memories. She had always planned on scanning them onto one of her flash drives, but now it was too late. All she had left was her memories. Why would someone do this to her?

As she sat there feeling sorry for herself, Terrance, or Ter, as he liked to be called, came into the office. She had been working with him for several months and they both had done a couple interviews on the General. The story on his country and the trade negations he was involved with was a big one and it was a credit to both of them to be assigned to it.

"Hey, baby, how's it hanging?" Ter bounced in, his usual jolly self. "This place is a mess, you throw a fit again?"

Ter loved teasing her and their relationship was a good one. They were friends, but nothing more. Dottie didn't know for sure, but she thought he was gay.

"Hey, you, I thought you made this mess," she answered him, trying to smile through her tears.

He walked up to her, giving her a big hug, then looked Derek up and down. He knew Derek from several activities at the White House and they were comfortable with each other, even though Derek knew little about him.

Shaking hands with the man, he gave Ter and Dottie some space, knowing if they could talk and compare notes, he would get his answers quicker and they could get out of there.

Tyler walked up to where he was standing and told him that Preston had been escorted off the property by internal affairs. Seemed the man had been getting his nose in places it didn't belong.

The video camera that was supposed to have been recording activity in Dottie's office had been disabled during the time of the break-in and things were beginning to look like an inside job.

Derek listened to Tyler's report and nodded his head. They couldn't catch a break on this one. Between his team, the FBI, and local yokels, everyone in the building had or was being interviewed. The situation was as under control as it could be.

Running his hands through his hair, a gesture he did when he was frustrated, Derek walked back to where Terrance and Dottie were still talking.

She was smiling when Derek walked up and reached for him. "I was just telling Ter about how we've been spending time together," she said, grasping his hand and pulling him closer to her.

He slipped an arm around her and pulled her to stand. "If you've done all you can here, let's go and get out of here."

"There's not really much more I can do except clean up and Matt hired a crew for that. Ter, catch you later." She talked to a few more people as they walked out and he drove her to her condo so they could check out what the crew had been able to accomplish. She hadn't seen it since it had been broken into.

Chapter Thirteen

Dottie hadn't been back to her condo since the night she had seen it trashed. The change was remarkable. Except for a few things that were out of place, it looked like nothing had ever happened. Most of her pictures had been restored and the picture of her mother looked perfect. Tears started streaming down her face as she walked through to all the rooms. It was perfect.

Turning to Derek, she threw her arms around him. "Thank you, I don't know what I would have done without you to lean on these past few weeks, you've been my rock." *And I'm starting to depend on you too much.* She didn't say this last out loud, but the more she thought about it, it was true.

She had never tried to depend on anyone but herself. She had found out the hard way that if you depended on other people too much, they either let you down or left you. So she had learned not to do that, but it was different with Derek. It just seemed natural to let him take charge. Maybe that was what he meant when he called her a natural submissive.

Derek took her back to his place. The next night was Saturday and there was some event going on at the club that he wanted to take her to. He again supplied the outfit, this time a light pink spaghetti-strap sheath, low-cut in the front and reaching barely to the top of her thighs. He had a matching thong and silver strappy stilettos to go with it. Dottie wasn't sure about the shoes. She was so tall she never wore anything but the lowest heels. She was sure she was going to break her ankle. When she told Derek as much, he just laughed and said, "Hang onto me, I'll keep you from falling." He probably had planned on it the whole time.

The event at the club was a collaring for two longtime members and friends of Derek, Trish Hamilton, and Norris Grant.

Dottie watched the ceremony in awe. It was beautiful and much more intense than a wedding ceremony. She had tears in her eyes by the end of it.

Derek explained everything that was happening to her as Norris fastened Trish into a pair of stocks. Club charter provided that at the end of every collaring ceremony the submissive (male or female) was secured into the stocks on stage for a duration of fifteen minutes to no longer than one hour to be determined by the Dom, and every Dom or Domme in the club was allowed to give them five swats on the buttocks with the implement of their choice. They were allowed to choose from implements provided by the Dom, so the submissive's Dom had some control over the procedures.

Norris had chosen to have Trish in the stocks for twenty minutes and provided a selection of paddles and straps for the Doms to use on Trish.

Derek and Dottie stood to watch for a few minutes before he led her to the bar.

"You're not going to congratulate her?" Dottie asked. She thought it was a weird way to congratulate someone, but not being in the lifestyle, figured it was normal.

"No, if I want to smack someone's ass, I have one right here to use." He grinned at her as he slapped her on the butt.

Grabbing her by the hand, he led her to the private rooms. Taking her to the room that was set up like a sultan's tent, he unlocked the door. "Change into what is lying on the cushions, I'll be back," he told her as he opened the door and let her in.

Instead of a bed, there was a large pile of cushions surrounded by gauze drapes that dropped from the ceiling and resembled a teepee.

Curious to see what he had planned, she anxiously went to change. In the past week, she and Derek had had many talks and she had told him of her fantasy to be captured by an evil sultan and how she wanted to be forced to submit to the wicked man's ways. Looked like she was going to be able to play that out tonight, she thought with a smile on her face.

Looking at the pile of pillows she found an aqua-green harem girl outfit. Dottie quickly put on all but the nipple clamps. As she was looking at them, Derek walked through the door. He was wearing a sultan's outfit, his robes matching her outfit. She almost clapped her hands in glee.

"I knew you would need help with those," he said, taking the clamps from her.

Dottie had forgotten she was holding them in her excitement. "Okay, Master, may I try something?"

Derek smiled and told her yes.

"You stay right there." She was barefoot and backed up to the far wall of the room. Taking a running start, she smiled a huge smile at Derek and said, "Catch me," as she took off running. Just before she got to him she leaped, wrapping her arms around his neck and legs around his waist.

Laughing, he wrapped one arm around her waist and angled the other over her back to cup her head. Just before kissing her, he asked, "What was all that about?" Then he took her mouth with his, exploring all that she was.

When he let her up for air, she laughed and said, "I've always wanted to do that, but was afraid to. I knew you could and would catch me. I may greet you like that often." She was giggling like a schoolgirl.

Holding her tight, he walked her over to the large overstuffed chair in the room and sat, still holding her. "Honey, you can do that anytime you want. I will always catch you." And he kissed her again, and again.

They played sultan and slave girl that night. Dottie had never felt as carefree. By the end of the evening, she was screaming from all the orgasms Derek had given her and was so exhausted, he had to carry her to the truck and into the house.

The weekend was quiet and Monday brought reality again. Dottie had to go to work. She needed to work with Terrance on the General's story and there were several other matters she needed to attend to.

Derek drove her to her office, but had a meeting at headquarters, so he left her in the care of several members of the team.

There had been several more disappearances over the last few weeks and the pressure was coming down on him. No one could figure out how the General was doing it. No one was talking and the women that were disappearing were no longer just hookers and homeless teenagers. Now girls from the local colleges were going missing. No one ever claimed to see anything.

Stressed after his meeting, Derek wanted to find Dottie and have lunch. He radioed the team to check her location, only to find that she and Terrance were on assignment at the White House and would not be available for several hours.

At loose ends, he decided to go over her personal flash drives again just in case the team had missed something.

Reviewing the folders again, he found one that was password encrypted. Trying all the passwords Dottie had given him, nothing worked. She had been so free with all the information they had needed, why would she hide this one file? Looking at the file info, it didn't come from the same source as any of the other files. Something was up.

Trying the team again, he was informed that Dottie was still with Terrance at the White House and decided to go there. Packing his laptop so that he could work while he waited, the hairs on his neck started to stand up. Something was up.

When he got to his office, he called Dillon, the team's computer expert, to come talk with him. He knew and could do a lot with computers, but Dillon was amazing and nothing got by him. He was sure that Dillon had already found the file and was working on it.

Dillon reported in and as Derek was already aware, had found the file and was working on finding the password. He had already spoken to Dottie about it and she had no knowledge of the file or how it got onto her flash drive. It was on the flash from her laptop and since she sometimes left the laptop at the office when she didn't need it at home, any number of people could have gotten access to it.

Dillon and Derek worked on the file for over an hour before Dillon finally cracked it. They had used all the passwords Dottie had given them and none of them had worked, but finally Dillon had written a program that took all the passwords from the people in Dottie's office and tried them in different combinations until the file opened.

When Derek and Dillon looked at the file, they were astounded. It was a list of woman's names and ages, a dollar amount, and a delivery date:

Pam Newsome 20 $15,000 7/25/14
Evelyn Tart 19 $225,000 7/31/14
Nancy Smith 18 $315,000 6/22/13
Carla Trane 22 $125,000 5/15/14

And so on until the last name on the list was Dorothy Chapman. The price next to her name was one million dollars and the delivery date was today's date. Derek immediately radioed the team. He didn't care what they had to interrupt. He wanted eyes on her now.

It wasn't long before he had the answer he already knew. Dottie was nowhere to be found. The meeting she had been involved in was continuing, but she and Terrance were not there.

A quick questioning of the group revealed that they had left when the group broke for lunch and never came back to the meeting.

Derek questioned the team. Who had fucked up this time? Trent Clark and his partner from the FBI, David Davis, had followed the van that Dottie and Terrance took to lunch. Everything seemed on the up and up. They watched Dottie and Terrance go and eat and then get back in the van. They then followed them back to the White House and saw them leave the van and return to the meeting room. They did not follow them into the meeting.

Derek then concluded that Dottie had disappeared somewhere in the White House. There was any number of exits they could have left out of. Luckily, there were video cameras on all exits and parking lots, and all the roads around the building were also on camera. All they had to do now was look at the footage. There were over a hundred cameras in all to watch, but they had an approximate time.

Dillon quickly wrote a computer program to scan all the video for the correct timestamp and the team sat at several monitors to watch.

Within the first few views, Tracy saw it. Terrance had Dottie's arm twisted behind her back and was dragging her out to a parking lot. Quickly pulling up the corresponding camera for the parking lot, they saw Terrance force Dottie into a black SUV with dignitary license plates, and it appeared that there were at least two more men in the van.

Following the SUV on various cameras took some work, but in a relatively short time, Dillon was able to combine all the footage onto a continuous tape and they could watch from the time she was kidnapped until she was taken on a road that led out of town.

The team quickly pulled maps, trying to figure out where she might have been taken.

Knowing all dignitaries' cars were equipped with GPS and tracking devices, Dillon quickly started tracing the SUV.

Derek ran to his own SUV, and he and Tyler began pursuit. The kidnappers were over an hour ahead of them and Derek prayed that they had not been able to get Dottie on a plane out of the country yet. The team fed them directions as they drove, and Derek nearly killed them, getting them out of town, to the point that Tyler was ready to take over driving...at gunpoint, if he needed to.

Finally convincing Derek that getting them killed would not help Dottie, Derek slowed a little, but his control was on the edge. Not something a Dom wanted to admit.

Derek and Tyler planned their attack as they drove. The team was soon following with a contingent of FBI, more Secret Service, and local law enforcement. All they needed was the Marines and they would have a complete battalion.

Tyler updated the team on the plan and everyone, including the locals, was ready to go. Tracking the kidnappers to a deserted airport, they stopped several yards away from the lone hangar and proceeded on foot.

The group surrounded the hangar, and on a pre-designated signal stormed the hangar. It was risky, but without knowing how many antagonists there were and how they were armed, it had been agreed that a blitz attack was the best way to go.

Since Dottie was the one likeliest to get hurt, Derek and Tyler were going straight for her and anyone that might be near her. The remainder of the group would take care of anyone else. They had to hope that they didn't have her on the plane yet or everything changed.

Chapter Fourteen

It was over before Dottie realized what was going on. One minute she was preparing herself for the torture they had been threatening her with and the next she was in Derek's arms.

The idiots who had taken her all dropped to the ground without a fight the minute the attack began, all except Terrance, who immediately jumped behind Dottie and started to act like he was also a victim. Everyone knew better and he was soon in custody with the other idiots.

Derek quickly freed Dottie and carried her out of the chaos and into his SUV. Sitting her in the seat, he wrapped her in his suit jacket and held her tight. Hysterically crying, she buried her face in his chest and let it all go. She had been strong as long as she could. Derek was here now. There was no longer any need to fight it.

Once she had calmed, Dottie told Derek how Terrance had drugged her at lunch, and by the time they got back to the White House, she was so woozy that she couldn't fight.

They had bundled her into the waiting vehicle and during the ride to the hangar, threatened her with torture and removed her suit and shoes, leaving her in her thin chemise and underwear. When they got her to the hangar, she struggled so much that it took four of them to tie her to the chair.

By the time Dottie had finished telling her story to Derek, he had managed to lift her and was sitting in the seat, holding her in his lap. He knew Tyler would be out soon and would drive them back to his place. His job for right now was to hold and comfort his woman.

Derek buried Dottie's face in his chest as they brought her kidnappers out, not wanting her to see. It was bad enough that she was going to have to retell the story several more times before she was done. Right now all he wanted to do was to get her home, into a hot bath, and into his bed where he could hold and comfort her.

Tyler had them home in record time and promised to let Derek know what was going on. The nightmare wasn't over, but it was close. Dottie would still have to be debriefed and testify at Terrance's and the other kidnapper's hearings, but with the file they had found on her drive, Terrance would not be able to deny his involvement.

Tyler called Derek later that evening to let him know that the list of names he had found could be matched up with missing women in the area and that they were doing their best to notify families and track down the whereabouts of the women. One of the kidnappers was talking, hoping for a lighter punishment, so they had some leads. It was going to be slow going, but it looked like there might be some good outcomes. Derek waited to tell Dottie the good news, not wanting to disturb the rest she was getting.

He hadn't left her side since he got her home, and even as he talked to Tyler, he lay in bed beside her. Ending the call, he turned his phone off and pulled Dottie to him. The debriefing would wait until she was in better condition. She had told him her story and he would remember every word for the rest of his life.

Dottie woke the next morning and she was lying on top of Derek, skin to skin. Everything that had happened yesterday seemed like a terrible, terrible nightmare. Unfortunately, it was a real one. She shuddered at the thought of what could have happened had Derek and the others not stormed in when they did, thanking her lucky stars that they did appear in time.

Leaving her head on his chest, she snuggled, trying to get even closer, wishing she could crawl in his skin with him. She didn't know how, but in the short time they had been together, he had become her rock. She couldn't imagine her life without him and hoped he felt the same.

She could tell when he woke up, the slight stirring as his breathing shifted from sleep to wakefulness, the rise in his body temperature, his hand sliding across her ass...all these things let her know he was awake.

She lifted her face to his, planning on giving him a "good morning, I love you" kiss, but before she could, he flipped her over to her back.

"Hey, baby," he said as he loomed over her, caging her body with his, and took her mouth in a branding kiss.

Pulling back, he looked deep into her eyes and said, "I've never been as scared as I was yesterday. I should paddle your ass for putting me through that." And he took her mouth again.

Dottie wrapped her arms around his muscular back, holding tight, he was her lifeline and she needed him to take her now. She needed his strength, his dominance, needed him to take what was his and envelop her with his maleness. She needed him.

"Derek, take me, tell me who I belong to, make me yours, and never let me go."

At her words, he fitted himself to her and slammed in. She was his and he was never going to let her go.

It was a rough fucking, that was all it could be called. He branded himself on her, spoiling her for any other man. No one, no one would ever take what was his again. Again and again, he slammed into her, growling the word "Mine!" with every inward thrust. Her answering "yours," just spurred him on. It had never been like this before for either of them, and they had their entire lives to show the depth of their love.

Both of them going over the edge, he fell to his side, pulling her with him. Panting, he told her, "If you ever, ever scare me like that again, I will paddle your ass so red you won't sit for a week. And don't think you're off the hook for yesterday. I think once I get my breath back, you are going over my knee."

Smiling, she ran her hand over his chest and answered, "Yes, Sir, whatever you want."

"Damned right," he said and took her mouth again.

It was several hours and a long spanking later before Derek let Dottie up again, but not before he asked, "Dottie, this probably isn't the most romantic proposal, but will you marry me? I promise to protect you with my life if necessary and share everything I have and am with you. Please say yes."

Even though he had just finished paddling her ass red and she was still hanging upside down over his lap, Dottie smiled. "Oh no, Mister, you are so not getting away with that. You flip me around and ask me properly or the answer's a big fat no." There was no way she was going to say no, but there was also no way she was answering him in this position.

Flipping her over and holding her in his lap, he looked into her mirth-filled eyes and said, "I suppose you want it all—nice dinner, me on one knee, a ring, the whole nine yards?" he asked, cupping her face.

"Yes, Sir, I want it all. I think I'm worth it, aren't I?"

"Baby, you're worth all that and more, but please don't make me wait. I promise, I will take you somewhere nice and I already have a ring, but please answer me." He had that little boy grin on his face and his eyes were pleading.

Dottie couldn't help but answer, "Yes, Derek Moore, I will marry you and be yours. I don't care about a ring and all the other things, I just want you." She smiled and pulled his head down to hers to seal the deal with a kiss.

When he let her up, she asked, "Do you really have a ring? Can I see it? When did you get it?"

Derek flipped her to the middle of the bed and stood, going into one of his dresser drawers. "This was my mother's. Dad got her a new one several years ago, and she gave it to me to have when I found the right woman. If you don't like it or want something different, we can shop and we will have it sized," he said, kneeling in front of where she had moved to sit and opening the box.

The ring was beautiful. A single, solitary square-cut diamond. Dottie couldn't tell sizes, but it was large, and the band gold and simple. Perfect. Holding out her hand, she waited for Derek to slip it on her finger.

Derek looked into her eyes and slipped the diamond on her finger. It fit perfectly. They both smiled. Fate, it was meant to be.

Chapter Fifteen

They were married six months later. Dottie had spent her time getting to know Derek's sisters and family. She had cut back her hours at work and was not traveling anymore. Any traveling she would do would be with Derek, who had also cut back his hours at the Secret Service and was spending more hands-on time at the club, managing.

He was preparing to retire in the next six months to a year and was going to be managing the club full-time. He and Dottie spent many evenings there, playing or just hanging out. They had explored most of the theme rooms and Dottie was becoming more comfortable with herself and her submissiveness. She had started talking to several of the women who were at the club regularly and was becoming close friends with Tracy, the FBI agent who had conducted her first interview.

The trial of the men who had kidnapped her, including Terrance, was over and all had been convicted and were serving jail time. In a touching move, Terrance had personally apologized at his trial, admitting the money had lured him in.

Most of the women had been found and returned to their families. The General may have been an ass, but he kept impeccable records, which were instrumental in finding the women. The negotiations with his country were continuing, but with a different representative.

Dottie and Derek were happy and content. Dottie had planned a special dinner that evening. Derek was going to give her his collar and then she had a surprise for him. Their family was expanding. She was pregnant.

The End

Don't miss out!

Visit the website below and you can sign up to receive emails whenever Rose Nickol publishes a new book. There's no charge and no obligation.

https://books2read.com/r/B-A-QFBG-KPQNB

BOOKS2READ

Connecting independent readers to independent writers.

Also by Rose Nickol

All the President's Men
Derek's Darling Damsel

Club de Fleur
Club de Fleur 3: Theresa`

Club de Fleurs
Club de Fleurs: Jenna

Daddies on Patrol
His Little Waif

Heroes of the Heart
Rescuing Trent Heroes of the Heart 3

Standalone
Snow Angel

Watch for more at rosenickol.com.

All these conflicts lead to divided families where no one wants to speak to each other. What ever happened to compassion? Surely, parents taught their children to communicate with them while they were growing up. In my experience, it doesn't matter how much you foster trust, people are going to isolate themselves with their secrets.

You may feel like you have the most perfect children, but they're going to keep things to themselves. Sorry kids, your parents won't reveal everything from their past. So, that means someone is going to be upset by the secrets and eventually leave home without communicating for a long time.

The time away brings away about pain and unwanted suffering. Who wants to be the first to open the door to the heart? Can you allow what matters the most to be felt without condemnation? I'm talking about love. Do you love each other enough to forgive? I know how hard it is to do so at times, but we must turn the energy of distrust into an energy of unconditional love.

Parents generally take the first step, and children are usually resistant for a longer period. Believe me, time does heal wounds, especially if both parties agree to communicate. Children want acceptance and freedom to mess up. Even though parents know that messing up isn't always the best way to grow up; we just hope nothing bad happens to them while they try to figure life out.

Forgiveness, what a novel idea. I believe that God needs us to forgive each other for our own good. It is one of his mysterious tests that all of us must pass as often as possible. As a family, we are stronger together than apart. Let's strive to love each other more and become a family that forgives. Amen.

Chapter 5

Do Not Provoke Your Children

Ephesians 6:4
And you, fathers, do not provoke your children to
wrath, but bring them up in the training and
admonition of the Lord.

Are you a parent whose child is constantly mad at you for no reason at all? Or could it be that you did something that made your child so mad, that he or she is acting out all the time? I know using universal terms such as all the time is a bit much, but an angry child can make life seem like a broken record.

As parents we can provoke our children to anger if we say no to certain things in a way that makes our children feel unappreciated. Sometimes, we may raise our voices without realizing the impact on our children's self-esteem. Especially, if we have a strong-willed child who is destined for leadership. Some children need more explaining then others, because we can give them firm and direct answers that make no sense to them at all.

One of the things I know they don't like, and that's us telling them that, "when we were your age, we did..." Well, they see themselves as being in a newer and more updated age where things make more sense to them and not us. All the things we did back in the day isn't equal to the things they are dealing with today. I mean, they have more advanced technologies, music that doesn't make since to us, and social media apps.

Children today like to multi-task. They can talk or text while listening to music and playing a video game at the same time. I often observe my children wearing headphones, watching a YouTube video, and on their laptops at the same time while talking to each other.

I don't know about you, but these are the same children that we raised in church to be strong believers. Although they are overachievers scholastically, I wish they would stop prioritizing tech. When you tell them to put it away for a while, their worlds turn upside down. As a parent you must be firm. If one or all of them get upset at our responses, we just explain to them what idolatry is, and how damaging too much of something cool and unnatural can be.

Our goal as parents should be to communicate in a way that is influential and encouraging. Teach them the reverence of the Lord and show them a better way to do things. There should never be a reason to take things from them unless it is harming them. Build character in them and lay a strong foundation of love. Yes, they can take over the world, but without the right guidance, they're doomed to failure. And who will thcy most likely be upset with? You guested it, their parents.

Finally, try to use a calm voice to quiet their anger, and be confident. Speak to them in a way that shows that you love them and that you care enough to keep them focused. So, turn to God's word, and do what it says. Train your child in the way he or she should go, so that when they get older, they will not abandon His righteous ways. Proverbs 22:6. Amen.

Chapter 6

Honor Your Father & Mother

Exodus 20:12
"Honor your father and your mother, so that you
may live long in the land the LORD your God is
giving you.

This post is for all the children who haven't figured it out yet. And, for the parents who have children that made life seem difficult. Let me ask you a simple, but important question. Do you honor your father and mother?

One must understand that the answer to the question above holds the key to your future. Maybe, I should ask if you love your father and mother? Many of us would say "Yes" to that question. But, did you know that you can't separate love from honor without removing respect from the formula.

I tell my father and mother that I love them as often as possible; then I follow up with a visit or phone call on Mother's and Father's day, accompanied with a gift. Needless you say, birthdays and all holidays are included. You see, the constant contact and verbal affection is reinforced by their gifts.

Growing up I looked at my mom and dad as the queen and king of the house. I was taught to be generous and to give when necessary. My parents never forgot my birthday or Christmas. They made sure that I had food, clothes, and a place to stay. I was even allowed to play sports or whatever I wanted if it was appropriate and feasible.

School even tried to teach us to honor our parents by making sure we created handmade gifts for the appropriate occasions. Some of those gifts were awful looking, but our parents found them adorable.

Children, if you can remember your parents blessing you when you were younger; try blessing them now while they're still alive. Their only dream for you is to have a better life than the one they had. You should honor and respect them based on giving you life. Thank them for doing their best to protect you from the bad things and showing you the good things that make a difference in the lives of others.

Yes, you love your parents, but do you honor them in the way that the Lord has taught you in His word. Where do you think your love comes from? That answer should be very simple. God is love. Love never fails. And you can't honor your father and mother without true love. Love that only God can give.

God wants us to live long on this Earth. Long enough to see our children have children. He wants us to experience His love through watching our children love each other and passing that love onto their children. This honor and love thing should be a never-ending cycle.

Again, honor your father and mother. You will live long on this Earth. And, that honor

will live on through your children, and then
their children. Amen.

Chapter 7

Learn to Listen

Proverbs 6:20
My son, keep your father's command and do not
forsake your mother's teaching.

Are you listening? Really, are you listening?

In this world of constant distractions, we

tend not to listen or focus on the things that

are around us. Things such as the news,

small things that loved ones are doing, or

things that they are trying to say.

If you are a person who is easily distracted,

it may be because you never started your life

listening to others. Were you a child that

listened to your parents? Or, did you allow

what they were saying to you to go into one ear and out the other?

Sometimes we think that world revolves around us. Is that you? If so, let me remind you that you're supposed to listen to your elders; or in this case your parents. The reason is that they have years of wisdom to share with you. If you have good parents, I mean the kind that raised you in a loving and well structured environment; then you can relate to this blog post.

Your parents or legal guardians are full life-giving shortcuts. Some may not want to share their experiences, but they can share their opinions. It important to note: listen carefully to what they are not saying. Huh?

What do you mean? I mean you must read between the lines of their wisdom.

You may have the most intelligent parents in the world, but their wisdom may not fit into what you are doing now. Their years on this planet have been preparing them for all the levels in their lives. Now, before you say "huh" again, let me explain. Most children start off living similar lives to their parents because that's what they've been taught. In the long run they ultimately find their own way.

I remember the first moment I really listened to my mother. I was a teenager, growing up in St. Louis, Missouri. She took me to the new downtown mall for lunch. Before we left the mall that day, she had me sit down with her to enjoy the sun rays. Then she started talking about appreciating life. She really needed me to listen to her that day. She knew that I was destined to do things differently from my brothers. You know what? She was right.

The lesson of this blog is to listen to your parents, and you will know how to get your children to listen to you. Ahh! You thought I was going to tell you to live your life the way your parents want you to live it. Not at all, I want you to live your life the way God intended. Well, that's another story for later.

Chapter 8

God's Mercy

Ephesians 2:4-5

But because of his great love for us, God, who is rich in mercy, made us alive with Christ even when we were dead in transgressions—it is by grace you have been saved.

Have you ever experienced God's mercy? Or, did you recognize it when God was merciful to you? These questions are not always understood by someone who doesn't know what His mercy is. Well, let's define mercy. Mercy is the compassionate action offered by someone after you do something that is considered wrong. In other words, you do not receive a punishment or suffer consequences for your actions.

Mercy is often mistaken as love because it embodies love. Yes, in order to show mercy, you must be able to show love. For example, I saw an episode of one of my favorite crime shows; in which the FBI busted a lady for drug possession although the drugs belonged to her boyfriend. To make a long story short, after they arrested the boyfriend, they dropped the drug charges on her so she could raise her daughter. You see, mercy embodies love, compassion, and the big picture, hope for humanity.

God treats us the same way. He knows that we are going to sin and make mistakes. As hard as it is to be perfect; perfection or maturity requires something that we can't do by ourselves. Perfection comes from knowing God in a personal way through our

Lord and Savior Jesus Christ. God showed us mercy by sending His son Jesus to live as the greatest example the world has ever known. He died so that our sins may be forgiven.

Think about the last time you messed up on your job. Did you get written up or worse? Or, did they show you mercy? Did someone you know hurt you in a way that you felt was unforgivable? If so, did you show them mercy? It doesn't matter what the circumstance is, mercy is for everyone; especially if that person is penitent.

So, tell your family and friends about God's mercy. It is one of the most profound gifts you and I will ever experience. Share your experiences with others so that they can find

hope in tomorrow. As it says in the Bible,
"God's mercy endures forever..!"

Chapter 9

Only Believe My Child

Acts 16:31

Believe in the Lord Jesus Christ, and you will be saved.

What amazes me is that we have our children baptized when they're babies, raise them in the church, and later let them decide what to do with their lives once they're old enough to choose. I don't know about you, but doesn't it feel like time has a way of playing an ironic game with us?

I would like for you to remember that time in your life when you questioned your beliefs. You know that time between the ages of 10-13. A permanent lifelong question had to be asked, "Do I really believe in God?" You see, I asked that question when I was 11. That question had me looking for answers for days. If you're not a person that prays, you need to become one quick. It was if I was in a real-life tug of war. Sure, I lacked commitment during my teenage years, but I was determined to serve the Lord my God all the days of my life.

When I look back on those years, my mother never stopped putting God's word in front of me. I had Bible reading assignments everyday along with my schoolwork. She knew that those were the questionable years. Yes, our children have doubts and question God's word; but my question to you is, are you there for your children when they have questions on faith?

With all the options presenting our children today, we have to be alert and ready to help with the confusion. Many of us have been quiet for so long, that our children think that they are experts concerning faith. I hope that what they have learned from us and in church will stay with them.

Philippians 1:6 And I am sure of this, that he who began a good work in you will bring it to completion at the day of Jesus Christ.

My mother reminds me of this scripture all the time. It reminds me that I must trust that the Lord will look out for my children all the days of their lives. I can be at peace because

I did my part in introducing them to God. Now, they must willfully choose Him as their Creator.

So, you can also rest assure that God will always look out for your children. Just tell them to only believe, only believe my child! It will work out. Keep the faith my friends.

Conclusion

I am a firm believer in life is what you make it. God has given us all the things we need in His word. The truth is that we should continue to trust in Him as parents and work together for better days. I can only ask women to allow their children's dads to be contributing fathers. Have a well-structured Godly home.

Everyone's circumstances are different. But if you have a good father figure for your children; give that man the chance to prove that he can be the head of the household. No one is perfect, but with God's guidance everyone can benefit. Start loving each other with a true purpose. Put God first and make our children "Great!"